THE CLUE OF THE BRILLIANT BASTARD

REMINGTONS OF THE REGENCY
BOOK THREE

ELLIE ST. CLAIR

CONTENTS

Facebook: Ellie St. Clair

Cover by AJF Designs

Do you love historical romance? Receive access to a free ebook, as well as exclusive content such as giveaways, contests, freebies and advance notice of pre-orders through my mailing list!

Sign up here!

The Remingtons
The Mystery of the Debonair Duke
The Secret of the Dashing Detective
The Clue of the Brilliant Bastard
The Quest of the Reclusive Rogue

For a full list of all of Ellie's books, please see
www.elliestclair.com/books.

CHAPTER 1

*M*aria could not stop shaking.

She fisted her hands together, wrapping her fingers tightly around one another, feeling the hateful ring biting into her skin. She longed to rip it off, to throw it across the church along with the vows that had just been uttered from her very own lips.

But it was too late. It was done.

She was married.

She couldn't look up at the man next to her. She hardly knew him and wondered if she should have attempted to become better acquainted with him before they had actually wed — although it was a little late for that now. He had courted her as was expected, yes, but it had been nothing more than a dance when they attended the same event, tea with her mother present, and a ride through Hyde Park. It was all a farce, if anyone were to ask Maria.

But, of course, no one did.

She smiled woodenly at all of the people who had gathered in St. George's to witness the carefully contrived match. One that her parents were ever so pleased with, especially

1

when they had despaired of their daughter ever finding a respectable husband after she had been turned aside by a duke for a woman most considered quite odd and not at all marriageable.

Maria actually quite liked Lady Emma — now the Duchess of Warwick — but of course, that was of no consequence to anyone either.

So, she did what she always did. She smiled and nodded.

All in attendance seemed quite approving of the match. All but her friend, Juliana, who stared at her now with the same concern she had expressed before the wedding, concern that Maria had tried to brush away.

She couldn't have said how she walked down the aisle, out of the church, and climbed into the carriage with the help of her husband's gloved hand, but suddenly she realized she was sitting within it on the squabs, alone with her husband. A stranger.

He leaned toward her, coming perilously close to her face. She tried not to visibly bristle at the warmth of his breath on her cheek, nor the odour that accompanied it, which she felt was akin to cheap wine mixed with salmon that had gone putrid and sat in the icebox for far too long.

"Alone at last."

Maria swallowed hard, keeping her gaze on the top of the squab across from her, wishing she was sitting upon it and not beside the man who was now her husband.

Her husband. How was it that despite the fact this had been expected of her for her entire life, it still seemed such a foreign concept?

Before she knew what was happening, his large hand was on her thigh, squeezing, rising along her leg, and Maria held her breath as she willed him away — but of course, that did nothing to stop him, as his hand ran higher until—

"Stop!" she yelped, jumping away across the seat.

She slapped a hand over her mouth when she caught her husband's glare. His eyes were harsh, his lips curled into a snarl, and the face that most in society considered handsome became twisted into a villainous expression that made her cower into the corner like a scared animal.

"I-I'm sorry," she stammered before he could say anything. "I was startled, and th-this is all quite sudden, and I—"

She didn't know what else to say. For she knew what she was supposed to do. Her mother had carefully and awkwardly explained what the expectations of her husband would be. Maria's stomach had churned at the thought of having to give control of her body to a man she didn't even know, but her mother had been very clear that she had no other choice.

But now that it was about to become reality, her acceptance of the fact no longer seemed as rational as it had been while sitting in her own bedroom contemplating what was to come.

"You are my wife," her husband bit out, advancing on her once more. "I can do as I please, and there is nothing that you have to say about it. Do you understand me?"

Maria, always one to quickly agree to what was spoken to her, found that for once, she didn't have it within herself to accept what he said.

"I-I understand. However, perhaps, I could have some time."

"Time for what?"

"To become accustomed to being married. To come to know you better. To—"

To her surprise, he let out a laugh. Only it wasn't a laugh of mirth. It was a long, cruel laugh, one that told her he would have no mercy on her, would not accept anything she had to say.

He leaned in close to her once more. "I'm not sure what you think this is all about," he said, "but I will have what I want, when I want it. Now, since you have not allowed me a taste, I shall have much more pent-up... desire tonight. You can have your *time*. But it runs out when the sun goes down."

Then he grinned, a slow, evil spreading of his lips that sent shivers all the way down Maria's spine.

Perhaps she was imagining things. Her husband was a man of rank, one who society accepted and seemed to admire. He certainly looked the part of the English gentleman with his light, perfectly coiffed curled hair, side-burns sculpted to an exacting length, and crisp, expensive clothing.

Was this how every bride felt in anticipation of what was to come on her wedding night? But then she remembered asking her friend, Juliana, about what she should expect. Juliana's smile had been nothing short of smug and saucy, as she told Maria that coming together with a man one loved was more than she could ever have dreamed.

But Juliana had chosen her husband. She had risked everything for him, as he was nothing more than a detective and she the sister of a duke. Maria knew she could never be strong enough to do the same.

A niggling thought tugged at her — one of a certain physician, the son of a duke, yes, but a bastard son. One who she had only met a couple of times, but who had made her heart beat faster than it ever had before.

But he was not for her. No, her father had promised her to Lord Bradley Dennison, and whatever Maria had thought she had desired was no longer an option.

For she was now Lady Dennison, and it was too late for her.

All she could do now was obey.

* * *

"Hudson?"

Hudson Lewis had just finished tidying his tools following the visit with his previous patient. As a physician, he was expected to simply diagnose, but he preferred to take more of a hands-on approach than most of his peers. For major operations, he referred his patients to a surgeon, one he trusted, but if it was a small ailment he could treat himself, he would do so.

"Yes?" he responded to his mother, who often accompanied him on his visits, assisting him as necessary. She had followed him home, as she often remained until he was most likely to be finished for the day.

She opened the door of the small study he used as his office, her greying head poking through. "Do you have a moment?"

"Of course."

She slipped through the door as though she was attempting to surreptitiously hide from someone, closing it quickly behind her before leaning back against it.

"You have a visitor," she said, her voice so low that it was near to a whisper.

"That is the nature of my business," he couldn't help but say wryly, and she shot him a glare. "And part of your role here is to assess who has come to fetch me. Is the case urgent?"

"Not a patient. A *visitor*."

Hudson eyed her with fond annoyance. "Would you care to tell me who it is?"

"It's one of *them*."

"I am assuming from the vehemence in your voice that it is a member of the Duke of Warwick's family."

"Somewhat."

He sighed, about to tell his mother to either come out and tell him what she wished to say or to leave and send in his next patient.

"It's Matthew Archibald."

The voice, however, was not his mother's. It came from the other side of the door and sounded a great deal like Archibald himself.

"Mother, the walls of this house are thin," he said, crossing his arms over his chest. Nor were the doors particularly thick.

His mother was correct, in a way, however. Matthew Archibald may not have been a member of the Remington family, but he was married to one of them — the duke's sister.

His own half-sister.

Hudson still had a difficult time believing that he was related to a duke and his family, that he was the son of a man who had been one of the most powerful in the country.

He had always known he was a bastard, however. That certainly hadn't changed.

"Come in, Archibald," he called out. The detective wasn't a bad sort, and despite his role in the investigation into the previous duke's death, he had risked everything to clear Hudson's name when the latter had been suspected of his murder.

"Lewis," Archibald said, reaching out to shake his hand, which Hudson took while his mother looked on with disapproval. He understood her hesitancy in trusting anyone related to the Remington family — she had been turned out years ago when she, a maid, had become pregnant with the duke's bastard — but she must understand that Archibald had none of the sins of the duke on his hands.

Archibald had simply been hired to look into his death,

and in the process, had fallen in love with one of the man's daughters.

"Is this a social call?" Lewis asked, raising an eyebrow. As much as he enjoyed Archibald's company, he did have patients to see.

"You could say that," Archibald said, casting a glance over at Hudson's mother, but she remained rooted to the spot, apparently not leaving until she knew what Archibald was here to say. "I come with an invitation as well as a message."

He held a note out to Hudson, who took it from his hand. He scanned the message before looking up at Hudson with raised eyebrows.

"The Duchess of Warwick invites me to a ball?"

"She does," Archibald said, ignoring Hudson's mother, who let out a snort that was not only undisguised but clearly on purpose for him to hear.

"No thank you," Hudson said, handing the invitation back, but Archibald raised his hands in the air.

"That is why I'm here. With the note plus a message. Emma understands why you might not want to come, but the entire family wanted you to know that they would very much appreciate your presence at the event. I know there was the unfortunate circumstance—"

"They accused my son of murder!" Hudson's mother burst in, and Hudson closed his eyes for a moment and pinched the bridge of his nose.

"Mother," he said as gently as he could, "perhaps Mr. Archibald and I might have a moment alone to discuss this."

"But—"

"I promise you I am perfectly capable of speaking for myself."

She let out a "humph," but finally left the room, which allowed Hudson a sigh of relief.

"She does not have the best delivery," Hudson said to

7

Archibald, "but she is right. The family — the duke in particular — did accuse me of murder. Despite evidence that spoke otherwise."

"I know," Archibald said, "but it was primarily the duke's accusations."

"And his mother's."

"That is true. But Juliana, Emma, and Prudence — as well as their grandmother, Lady Winchester — were all very much in support of you."

"For which I am grateful. But I hardly think society will willingly accept my presence."

"That, I understand," Archibald said, lifting his hat and raking a hand through his straight, light brown hair. "As it happens, there is an event ongoing today that I am not invited to myself, being a detective and all and not appropriate company."

"Oh?" Hudson said, though not at all interested. "Did Juliana attend without you?"

"She did," Archibald said with a nod, no emotion on his face. "She didn't want to, in protest for my omittance from the guest list, but we both knew how much her presence meant to Lady Maria and—"

"Lady Maria?"

Hudson couldn't stop his reaction as his head snapped up at mention of her name.

Archibald's eyebrows rose and Hudson cleared his throat as he turned his back and made a farce of tending to his instruments once more.

"I made Lady Maria's acquaintance some time ago," Hudson said, "and have not seen her in a few months. She was very... polite. I wondered how she was getting on."

He was well aware that it was far too much of an explanation, but once he had started his ramble, he wasn't sure where to stop.

8

"Yes," Archibald said, as Hudson turned his head over his shoulder to look at him. "It was her... event after all."

"Her event?" Hudson said, feigning nonchalance.

"You could call it that," Archibald said, pausing for a moment before telling him the truth of it all. "Lady Maria is getting married today."

CHAPTER 2

*M*aria stood in the middle of what was now her bedchamber, staring blankly at the ornately decorated walls around her. The dowager countess had made a great fuss about the fact that she was vacating her suite of rooms to make room for Maria. Maria would have been grateful had the dowager countess not made it abundantly clear that she had done so quite unwillingly, even though it was expected.

At the moment, Maria would have preferred to be anywhere *but* this suite of rooms, which not only connected to the earl's chamber but was also far too opulent for her liking. She enjoyed pink and cream and décor that spoke of comfort and home. Not these garish clashing colors of red and orange, gold and turquoise which swept around the room, accented by paintings that Maria had been told were the works of masters but were scenes showcasing death and tragedy.

Perhaps it was an echo of the dowager countess' own life. A life that would now be Maria's.

She sank down now on the edge of the bed. The wedding

breakfast had been worse than she would have imagined, with her husband sending her knowing, leering looks from across the table as he imbibed cup after cup of whatever drink it was that he preferred. She knew she should learn his preferences, but she couldn't find it within herself to care. Neither her family nor his own made any comment when his speech became slightly slurred, nor when his manners dropped a noticeable step.

Maria tried to remember if he had ever acted in such a way in her company previously. She could not recall a time, but then, she had not been in his presence for many meals.

His mother seemed to find herself more important than everyone at the rest of the table put together, while his sister, Lady Christina, was the sort of woman who men seemed to enjoy but women most often skirted with a wide berth whenever she came near.

Maria knew how much Juliana loathed the woman, for Lady Christina had taken extra care to make Juliana's life miserable, but Maria herself had never been at the source of her barbs before — at least not to her face.

Her sly comments, however, had not gone unnoticed, and Maria told herself to stay as far from her new sister-in-law as was possible.

Which would prove difficult when living in the same house.

A soft knock at the door caused Maria's spine to stiffen, although she reminded herself that if it was her husband, he would likely have barged in through the connecting door instead of knocking politely.

If she was at home, it would likely be her mother, but of course she would have departed by now. Even if she had remained, however, it did not seem that any of her family had been particularly concerned about her thoughts or feelings when they had arranged this wedding. No, they had been rather proud of themselves for finding such a respectable man who would agree to marry a woman who had already been passed over once.

"Come in," she called, and smiled in relief when she saw a friendly face. It was her maid, Anne, who had accompanied her upon her move to the earl's residence. Maria's smile faded somewhat when she saw that Anne was not alone, but instead another young maid followed in behind her. She appeared to be of lower service by her dress, and she kept her head down, her hands folded in front of her.

"Is something amiss?" Maria asked, and Anne bit her lip as the two maids curtseyed to her.

"I was unsure whether or not to bring this to you, my lady," she said, stealing a glance at the other maid, whose head was now dipped so far down she was looking at the floor, the top of her mobcap all that Maria could see, "but I heard some of the maids talking, and I could not help but ask questions. This is Jane."

"Good evening, Jane," Maria said politely, although she was quite confused. Whatever could a young maid in a household she had just joined want from her? "What can I help you with?"

"I want no trouble, my lady," Jane said, and Maria sat back down on the bed so she could at least partially see the girl's expression. "Anne said you would want to know."

Maria turned her gaze to Anne, concerned by the way her maid was looking at her. Anne's mother was Maria's own mother's lady's maid, and she had practically grown up in the house until she was old enough to start to work herself. Maria knew their relationship was rather odd, closer than most between lady and lady's maid, but she relied on Anne for far more than just styling her hair and fastening the back of her dress.

Anne took a deep breath before she finally told Maria why they were there.

"Jane has had quite a few... encounters with Lord Dennison. Encounters that she would prefer to avoid. And she is not the only one, although many of the maids have already left because of it."

"Of what nature are these encounters?" Maria asked, her heart racing, as she feared she already knew what was to come.

"He has forced his... attentions on many of the comely maids. Jane says many of them have left for other employ, because it is not only that his attentions were unwanted but that they were also cruel."

Maria swallowed. "In what way?"

Jane finally lifted her head, and when she met Maria's gaze, Maria shivered at the fear in her eyes.

"He enjoys nothing more than to see a woman in pain, my lady. And he will use whatever means necessary to ensure that maximum pain is found. I want no trouble, my lady, I truly do not, but you seem kind and Anne felt it was best to warn you. We've learned to fake the pain as early as possible and then it's not nearly so bad."

Maria's heart broke for the girl, then, and when she crossed the room to take her hands in hers, Jane looked up at her in shock.

"Why do you stay?" Maria asked earnestly. "Would it not be best for you to go, to find another placement?"

"The family is desperate for servants, now that so many have left. He said he would make sure that I would never get another reference, that he would tell any others who wanted to hire me the worst of stories. I need this job, my lady. I support my ma with it, for she is ill and—"

"I understand," Maria said, squeezing her hands as she

shared a look with Anne, whose eyes had widened considerably as she seemed to understand what this meant for not only Maria but for herself as well. "I know it is likely not possible for you to leave this moment, but if you can find another position, I promise that I will provide you the reference that you need."

"You will?" Jane asked, the slightest bit of hope entering her eyes.

"Of course," Maria said, forcing a smile on her face to hide the growing panic within her. For she could help Jane, but that wouldn't stop the earl. "Consider it my thanks for your bravery in coming to me."

Jane curtseyed once more before hurrying out the door. Anne looked at Maria with matching panic in her expression.

"My lady," she said softly, "what are we going to do?"

Maria set her jaw as she looked over at Anne, knowing there was only one option.

"I have no choice," she said. "But you do. I must stay, but you should return to my parents' residence."

"I cannot leave you," Anne said, although her words lacked conviction.

"You can," Maria said, hiding her desperation at the thought of being completely alone. "You have to. I have no choice in the matter. Not anymore. You, however, do. You have your life ahead of you, Anne, and you cannot let a man like Lord Dennison ruin it for you. For he will. You are a beautiful girl, and he will not allow that to go unnoticed. Help me disrobe and then pack your bags and call a hack."

"My lady," Anne began, pity in her gaze, but Maria shook her head.

"It's fine," she said even though it was anything but.

"Would you... would you leave as well?" Anne asked, wrinkling her nose. "I know you could not return home, but I would go with you, wherever you choose to go. You could start a new life. One away from here. You would not have the same comforts, but if he is truly so cruel, perhaps you would be better off."

"I cannot," Maria said immediately. "What would I do? I have no skills besides watercolor, needlepoint, and pouring tea. I have nowhere to go, no one to help me."

"Surely there must be someone."

A face that Maria had been trying to forget since she last saw him flashed across her mind, but she forced it away, for she could have nothing to do with it — with him. Her fate was sealed.

"This is my life," she said, attempting a smile as she turned her back so that Anne could help her undress. "Do not worry."

"Very well," Anne said, stepping forward and assisting her. "If you ever need anything, you know where to find me."

Maria nodded, stifling the sob that began to grow in her throat. When Anne finished, Maria couldn't help but reaching out and embracing her, requiring one last friendly touch before she resigned herself to what was to come.

She had no idea how long her husband would take to come to her. After attempting to read to pass the time but knowing that doing so was futile, she sat on the edge of her bed, nervously tapping her foot as she squeezed her eyes closed and did all she could to keep the panic from erupting as she waited — for the cruel monster the maids described, which Maria couldn't help but believe. She told herself to think of lovely thoughts while it happened, to do as Jane had suggested and express her pain before it became unbearable.

When the door connected to the dressing room finally opened, she jumped, unable to help the yelp that escaped from her lips.

The earl stepped through, shedding his jacket on the floor as he stepped toward her without a word. His stench of alcohol had only increased since she had left the party, and Maria immediately regretted the deep breath she took as she stood, hoping that, perhaps, he would treat his wife differently than he did other women.

Then he lifted the riding crop from his side, and she swallowed hard, stepping back in panic.

He grinned. "Do you know what it feels like to have this slapped on your skin?"

"I cannot say I do, my lord," Maria said, proud of herself for not letting him see the turmoil he caused within her. "I doubt it is pleasant."

He shrugged. "Some women like it. Others don't. Depends on how it is administered, I suppose."

"Perhaps... perhaps we can wait until another time to attempt such a thing?"

He smirked. "This is just the start, wife. Not to worry. I won't leave marks where anyone will see."

His waistcoat dropped to the floor now as he advanced toward her, and Maria couldn't help herself from shrinking back against the wall.

His hands came to his breeches, but then he stopped, muttering to himself.

"Is something amiss?" Maria couldn't help but ask.

"Best take a piss first. Don't move."

The second he was through the door and back to his own chambers, Maria stopped thinking. The time for that was past. She rushed to the window at the side of the room, throwing it open and allowing the cool night air to rush over her, chilling her even further than she was already by the fear that had crept in.

She leaned over the edge of the window, grateful her room was only on the first floor, although it was a fairly long drop to the small garden which faced the mews behind the house. She wasted a moment wishing that she was more like

Juliana, or even Juliana's sister, Prudence, who she knew would have no qualms about climbing down.

She didn't have much time to consider it, however, as she swung her leg over and began to creep down the trellis. It creaked under her weight, but she had far less fear of the trellis breaking than facing her husband in the room above.

She was nearly to the bottom when she heard a shout from the window above. She had no idea whether or not he could see her in the dark of the night, but he distracted her enough that her foot slipped and her ankle turned beneath her as her slippered foot hit the ground.

She bit her lip to keep from crying out before she ripped off her ring and threw it on the ground as she flew into the night as fast as the pain would allow her.

CHAPTER 3

*I*t had been a long day.

Hudson wiped his brow as he finished putting the last tool away and closed the cupboard. He hadn't finished with his final patient until well after dinner, and then his mother had returned with food for him. It was a blessing, but meant a light was on in his front window, which had invited one more patient who Hudson just couldn't turn away. Fortunately, he hadn't needed to leave his house that was more of an office than a home but had provided instruction and had promised to come check on the patient in the morning.

"I'm away for the night, son," his mother said, stepping into the doorway of his office.

"Thank you for staying late," he said, walking over and kissing her on the cheek. "I appreciate your help."

"You pay me well for it," she said with a laugh.

"Still, I couldn't do it without you."

"Speaking of," she said, her cheeks turning slightly pink, "next week I may take several days away, if that is all right with you?"

"Of course," he said immediately, although he was rather bewildered. Where could his mother possibly be going? She must have read the question on his face, for she continued in a stammering manner that was quite unlike her.

"I have a friend who suggested we leave the city for a time."

"I see," he said, wanting to know just who this friend was, but his mother was a grown woman who didn't need to explain herself to him. "Travelling outside of London is awfully expensive. Do you need any money?"

"No, no," she said, waving a hand and uncharacteristically backing out of the room in a hurry. "I will be just fine. Oh, and Hudson?"

"Yes?"

"You spend far too much time at work. Have you thought about trying to meet a nice young woman, settle down, begin a family?"

"Only every time you mention it to me," he said, but with a smile on his face, for he knew his mother meant well, even if she could pester him at times.

"It's just... I cannot be here helping you forever, and it would be nice to have someone else to assist you with the practice."

"I know, Mother, and I need you to know if the day comes when you no longer want to work here with me, I can hire someone else."

"What happened to not being able to do this without me?"

He laughed at that, shaking his head, but as he heard the front door of the house shut behind her, he contemplated her words. She was right. He should be settling down, finding a woman to spend the rest of his life with.

But something was holding him back. Only, he knew it wasn't a something — it was a someone.

Lady Maria Bennington.

A lady so far above him in station it was laughable. A lady who could never be his, one he could only admire from afar.

And now a married woman.

He sighed as he blew out the candle in the small study before continuing into his drawing room. He extinguished the candle in the front window as well before he poured himself a drink to sit with for a few moments in front of the fire before taking himself to bed.

He eased into the overstuffed armchair that had seen better days but in which he found far too much comfort to be rid of. He had just closed his eyes and taken a first sip of the brandy when he was startled by a knock on the door.

Hudson sighed, debated whether or not to answer it, and then stood as he knew he had no choice. His conscience wouldn't allow another decision.

"Doc?" came a voice as he swung the door open.

"Yes?" he answered, peering into the darkness, trying to determine the breadth of the man. As he stepped closer, he realized it was not that the man was overly large, but that he carried something in his arms. A woman, one limp and prostrate.

"Doc? Found someone."

"Smith, come in," Hudson said, waving the man in once he recognized his voice, knowing he could never turn away a person in such distress, as much as he longed for his bed.

He lit the candles once more, showing the merchant back through to the one place that made sense to place the woman — his bed. Smith laid the woman on the top of it, her long, flowing night rail hanging off the edge and draping to the floor.

"What seems to be the matter?" Hudson asked, as he stepped toward the woman, lifting the candle to cast the light over her body.

As he did, however, his breath caught, and he could not seem to will it to return.

For lying on his bed was none other than Lady Maria.

* * *

LIGHT BEGAN to filter through her eyelids, and Maria shifted as she tried to remember where she was, what had happened. She turned her head toward the light, but when she tried to open her eyes, her head began to ache something fierce, and she grimaced in response.

"Lie still for now," she heard a voice echo through her mind. The voice was soothing, one she recognized, which made her feel... safe. But who—

Suddenly the day's events came rushing through her mind, and she gasped as she remembered her husband, his approach to her bedroom, and what she had run from. Lord Dennison. His cruelty. The maids. Had he caught her? Was she back in his house? Was she... she couldn't help the whimper that escaped her lips, but before she could move, there was a hand on her arm.

"You're fine. You're safe. Just rest."

"But..." The light from behind her eyelids dimmed, and finally she was brave enough to open them a crack. A face swam in front of her, and she blinked a few times to try to focus. Not only was it familiar, but it was the face that had haunted her thoughts for weeks now. One rather like the Duke of Warwick's, but... softer, less pronounced cheekbones, his nose a touch smaller. He did, however, have the same dark hair, his eyes equally as blue although a slightly different shade. His build was trimmer, leaner, but there was a strength within him that Maria had sensed the first time she had met him.

"Doctor Lewis?" she managed, her voice coming out as a croak.

"It's me," he said, stepping toward her, placing a hand on her arm. "I've treated your ankle. It is a slight sprain as far as I can tell. You also appear to have sustained a head injury, but I'm afraid there is not much I can do for it but try to stop the external bleeding. I'd prefer not to try further measures unless I deem it necessary. Is your vision blurry? Do you feel that you might be—"

She wanted to shake her head, but her stomach revolted. He apparently anticipated it as he was ready with a pail. Maria was mortified but he did not seem disturbed.

"Better?" he asked, and she slowly, carefully, nodded her head.

"Good," he said. "Hopefully it is only a slight head wound that will heal shortly."

Maria lifted her hand to her head, surprised to find her hair had fallen around her shoulders, and there was a thick band of gauze wrap circling her skull.

She winced again. "What happened?"

"I was hoping you could tell me some of that," he said, "but first, if you are feeling well enough, would you prefer to sit in a chair out in front of the fire? You might be more comfortable than on the bed. If you feel faint, you can lie down again."

"Yes, please," she said, beginning to sit up, and he walked over and placed a hand on her back to help her rise. He held his other out to her, and she placed her hand in his with some hesitancy. She wasn't sure how she would feel about a man touching her at the moment, not after the threats her husband had made, but with Dr. Lewis, there was no hesitancy. Perhaps it was because he was a physician and dealt with patients every day. Or perhaps it was because one of her closest friends trusted him. Or perhaps it was just that he had a calming presence that reassured her. Whatever it was, she had no qualms about allowing his large, warm hand to wrap around hers and lead her off the bed and into the drawing room through the door.

He took her weight so she wouldn't have to put any on her injured ankle as she hobbled over to the chair in the corner of the main room. It didn't look like much but was surprisingly comfortable and yet also supportive. He sat across from her on a hard wooden dining stool.

"A friend of mine brought you to me," he began. "He said he found you not far from here, that he saw you running before you stumbled into someone else and then fell and hit your head against a brick wall. He had no idea that we were acquainted but brought you to me as I have this terrible habit of never turning anyone away, no matter the time of night. I apologize for examining you without your permission, but I wanted to ensure you had no other injuries beside the head wound."

She must have appeared somewhat stricken, for he lifted a hand and shook his head.

"You remained completely dressed, but I did check your arms and legs for any broken bones. I only found the sprain to your ankle. Did you sustain the injury at the same time?"

"I…" Maria found that she wasn't sure what to say. The night's events had returned to her with far too much clarity, but she was too ashamed to say any more. What was she supposed to tell this man who she had so much respect and admiration for — that she had allowed herself to be married off to a monster, and then when she had realized just how terrible he was, she had fled in the night, only to leave innocent young girls behind as victims?

He shifted in his chair before leaning forward, his hands clasped in front of him, his elbows resting on his knees.

"You do not need to tell me what happened if you don't

want to. I only ask because it helps me treat the injury if I know the nature of how it was sustained."

Maria felt all the more foolish. She cleared her throat.

"I fell. Not far, about a foot or two. But I was turning as I fell, which must have caused the twist to the ankle."

"That makes sense," he said, leaning back on the stool. He obviously had more questions, but she appreciated that he did not press her further.

"It is quite late," he said, getting to his feet. "I should really return you home. However, I heard... I heard that you were married today, so I wonder, just which home should I return you to?"

Panic began to beat wildly in Maria's chest as she remembered just where home was now. When she had fled, she had originally thought to return to her parents', but had quickly pushed aside the idea. No matter what she told them, they would have no choice but to return her to her husband. Not only that, but she would only have disappointed them with her disobedience. So instead, she had turned east. She had stumbled forward in a slow hobble until she had made it to Soho, when a family driving past in a cart had taken pity on her and allowed her a ride as far as the edge of Holborn. There, she had been twisted around as she tried to remember how to find Juliana's home. She knew she could trust her friend to take her in, and her husband, the detective, would be discreet.

But she had been overwhelmed by the unfamiliar streets, the filth on the ground, the people who filled the neighborhood at this hour. At some point, she must have fallen, which was when the man had found her.

How fortunate she was that he had brought her here.

"I cannot go home," she said softly now, and Hudson's eyes were so kind and understanding that she almost burst into tears right there.

"Would you like to tell me why?"

"I cannot. But just know I cannot return there. There is no place for me. I was married but... I will never go back there," she said, surprising herself with the vehemence in her voice. "Never."

"Very well," he said, his gaze hardening, although she wasn't sure why. "We best determine what to do with you, for tonight, at least. I could take you to stay with my mother, I suppose. She will ask questions as she is rather inquisitive, but she will provide you with a warm bed."

The thought of having to explain herself to Dr. Lewis' mother was nearly more than Maria could handle, and right now, the thought of leaving his side was rather frightening in itself. She had no idea why, but being close to him currently seemed to be of the utmost importance.

"I know this is a lot to ask," she said with some hesitancy, "but... could I stay here with you? Please?"

His eyes glinted for a second in a rather unfamiliar expression. She never should have asked. It had been far too forward of her. She wondered if she should retract her question, but then after a moment of hesitation, he met her gaze and nodded his head firmly.

"Yes," he said. "Whatever you need."

The relief that filled her was nearly enough to knock her over once more.

CHAPTER 4

*H*udson's house was rather small for a physician's — of that, he was well aware.

But it had never overly bothered him, until now, when he looked at it through Lady Maria's eyes.

It included the usual drawing room and dining area, his bedroom to the back, and the study to the other side. He supposed that could be used as a bedroom, but he preferred to keep his work as separate from his home as he could. A maid came once a day to clean and prepare dinner.

Overall, it was tidy, comfortable, and his mother had ensured that there was enough décor to make it presentable.

But it was so far from what Maria would be accustomed to that he couldn't imagine she would feel anything but pity for him.

He walked over to the window in front, looking one way and then the other before drawing the curtain shut tight in front of it.

"Are you concerned about something?" she asked him, obviously noticing, and he shook his head.

"Just that someone might see you. If it were ever discovered that you spent the night in my home, you would be ruined."

She let out a wry laugh. "It is far too late for that. This is the least of my worries."

The melancholy in her tone concerned him, as did the awareness of what might have happened to her. He didn't want to think about what her new husband could have possibly done that would cause her to flee in such distress.

He lit a few candles toward the back of the room and stoked the fire in the hearth before he showed her to the bedroom.

"You are likely tired, and I can imagine your head is sore," he said. "I will take one of the extra blankets and sleep in front of the fire. You can have the bed."

"Oh, no," she protested, "I cannot take your bed. I shall be perfectly fine in the drawing room."

He let out a low chuckle. "Absolutely not. But thank you for the offer. Tomorrow we shall have to determine the next steps for you, but for tonight, you have a bed and you are safe. Do you understand?"

Somehow, it became imperative to him that she know she had nothing to fear here with him. She needed his help, although whether she was more in need of a physician or a friend, he wasn't entirely sure.

"Lady Maria," he said, pausing in the doorway, "you do not need to tell me what happened, but as a physician, I must ask… are you hurt in any other way? Is there anything further that you require, that I would not have found in my examination?"

She turned a shade of pink as she looked down at the floor, unable to meet his eye.

"No," she said, her voice just above a whisper as she shook her head. "I could have been, it is true. But no, I am not."

"Good," he said, relief flooding through him with such an

intense feeling of protectiveness that he almost didn't know what to do with it. That this woman would trust him was so improbable he could hardly believe it, and yet here she was, in his home, in his bedroom, about to find her way under his blankets.

He swallowed hard as he pushed aside thoughts of her there, with him. She had obviously escaped a man who had threatened her and had sustained a head injury in the process. The last thing she needed was him standing in the doorway lusting after her.

"Are you hungry? Thirsty?"

"No, thank you. I'm fine."

"Very good," he said, pausing in the doorway, not wanting to leave her but knowing he must. "If you need anything, I am right out here."

"Thank you," she said, and with her soft smile following him out, he shut the door behind him.

* * *

AFTER THE DAY and night she had been through, Maria wouldn't have thought that she would ever be able to sleep.

Which was why she was surprised to wake the next morning feeling more rested than she had in days.

Perhaps it was because the anticipation of the wedding was gone. Now she was left with a situation she had to extricate herself from, it was true, but at least she no longer felt alone. Not with Dr. Lewis out there, waiting for her.

Dr. Lewis. What was she going to do? He had been so kind, so trusting, so unforceful about asking her to tell him all that had occurred, even though she knew he deserved answers. She could hardly stay here in hiding forever, could she?

She took a breath, looking down at herself in her dirty nightrail and wrapper. Goodness, what her mother would say to see her like this now. She could hardly believe it herself. But it was not as though she had any other choice. She had gotten herself into this mess. Now she had no choice but to get herself out of it.

It took her some time to first sit and then stand, a bout of light-headedness accompanying each action, and she summoned all the courage she had remaining before pushing the door open and then hobbling out into the main room, finding the sun was streaming in brightly through the wide window in front.

"Good morning."

Oh, goodness, her heart began to throb painfully at the sight in front of her.

For there was Dr. Lewis, framed by the front window, light streaming around him as though he had been sent here just for her. He held a cup in his hands, which he held out to her now.

"I wasn't sure if you preferred tea or coffee, but my best guess was tea, so I made a cup for you. You can add more sugar if you'd like. There are also some scones my mother left the other day. Hopefully they are still fresh enough."

Maria tried to hide her smile at the fact that he actually seemed a bit nervous, although why, she had no idea.

"Thank you," she said, reaching out and accepting his offering. "And thank you so much for allowing me into your home. I know it is a lot to ask."

"It's fine."

He held out a hand and led her to the small breakfast table. She appreciated the help and leaned on him harder than she meant to.

"Last night, I was trying to locate Juliana's," she said, the words tumbling out. "I got lost, and wasn't sure how to find my way there, but knew she and Matthew lived nearby. Perhaps... perhaps I could go to her today."

What she really wanted to ask, from deep within her, was if he would allow her to stay here, with him, but that was obviously an impossibility. He had a life of his own and the last thing he needed was a married woman who had completely ruined her own life to interrupt his and foist herself and her insurmountable problems upon him.

His eyes clouded for a moment, although with what, she wasn't entirely sure. Disappointment in her most likely. What must he think of her? First she had been spurned by his half-brother, a duke, and now here she was, in his home in nothing more than her night garments after running away from her marriage bed.

Although what he thought of her should be of no consequence. He was the half-brother of her friend, and now, she supposed, her physician of a sort, although she had no idea how she would ever pay him.

"I am happy to do whatever you would like," he said. "However, Archibald was here yesterday and informed me that he and Juliana were going to be visiting the country today — following up on a lead, he told me, although what it was and for which case, I am not entirely sure."

"I see," she said, furrowing her brow, although the knots in her stomach began to twist anew. If Juliana was gone, what was she to do? She supposed she could go to Juliana's sister, Prudence, although she didn't know her well. Then there was the duchess, formerly Lady Emma, but that was rather awkward being that she was originally supposed to have married her husband. Not that the duchess seemed to hold any ill will toward her, but still...

"I suppose..." she began, trying to find the right words. "I suppose I just need a few days to figure everything out then, perhaps until Juliana returns. I know this is a lot to ask, but would… could I… that is—"

"You are more than welcome to stay here," he said smoothly, and relief filled Maria.

"Oh, thank you," she said, pushing down the urge to jump up and throw her arms around him. "Thank you so much."

"Of course," he said with a nod, not showing what he really thought of it all, as Maria longed to ask him. "I will find you some clothing. In the meantime, we should ensure that no one knows you are here. I know you said there is nothing to fear, but I would hate to cause you any further scandal."

"My reputation means nothing anymore," she said, shaking her head too hard, forgetting for a moment the wound upon it and she lifted her hand at the surprise burst of pain. Goodness, what she must look like at the moment. "But yours is one well respected in the community. I would not want to ruin it due to your generosity toward me. I would, however, appreciate no one knowing I am here."

"Will people be looking for you?" he asked, fixing her with a level gaze.

"Likely," was all she could say.

"Very well," he said. "I must leave to begin my rounds, but I will be back as soon as I can — with clothing. There is some food in the larder for the day."

"Thank you so much," she said as tears sprang, unbidden, to her eyes, and she blinked rapidly to clear them. "I do not know what I have done to deserve your kindness, but—"

He leaned over and placed a hand on hers. "You have done nothing *not* to deserve it," he said. "Stay here. And don't open the door if anyone knocks."

She nodded, watching him go, already missing him until his return.

* * *

HUDSON DID all he could to push Lady Maria from his mind as he worked the rest of the day. He had to. If all he did was think of her, he would be far too distracted to properly see to his patients.

But even so, it was hard not to picture the soft tendrils of blond hair that curled ever so slightly around her shoulders, her blue eyes, the angelic glow that seemed to follow her around. She was every Englishman's dream, and she was sitting in his home in her nightclothes, which were now filthy but still expensive, as dirty as they were. Even with the bandage he had placed around her head, she was still the most beautiful woman he had ever seen. This entire scenario was so farfetched he wouldn't have believed it himself had he not known it to be true.

He only wished she would open up, let him in and tell him what had happened to her. He would do all he could to help — he just had to know how to do so.

Perhaps in time she would learn to trust him.

But that was all. As happy as he was to have her staying with him, it was also nearly torturous to have her so near and know that he could never come close, never have his arms around her or her lips on his. While her marriage may not be one that would ever be true in anything but name, she was still married, and she was still an English lady, daughter of a marquess, and wife of an earl if Archibald was correct.

Not a woman for him to even dream about.

Yet as he welcomed her into his home, she just took up further residence in his mind.

And he was helpless to prevent it.

CHAPTER 5

*H*udson and Maria fell into an easy rhythm over the next few days — perhaps a bit too easy, were he being honest with himself. They took tea together in the mornings before he would leave to see to his usual patients, spending all day looking forward to his return in the evenings. He would often come home during the day but would always be called out again before he could spend any proper time with Maria.

She would have dinner on the table each night, with the help of his maid. The girl was quite curious about Maria's presence, but they explained she was a friend in trouble. Dinner together was the first time in a long time that Hudson recalled actually coming home and enjoying a meal with another person, besides the odd dinner with his mother.

His mother was obviously quite distracted herself, such that she didn't notice, or at least made no comment regarding anything unusual about his house or his own actions. Whenever she arrived to begin the day assisting him, Maria made herself scarce in Hudson's bedroom so that she wouldn't have to explain her presence to his mother. But tonight, his mother had insisted that she was going to have dinner with him before she left on her mysterious sojourn, so Hudson knew that they had to come to a decision as to just who to trust in this ruse.

"Lady Maria," he called out as he walked through the door after his last patient, finding her at the counter in the back of his house, cutting an assortment of vegetables. She was wearing a pale yellow dress, one that flattered her even if it was far from the expensive cuts and fabrics she would be used to wearing. He had enjoyed choosing the fabrics at the seamstress, as awkward as he had felt in the shop.

"Dr. Lewis," she greeted him with a cheery smile, one that he knew would never cease to warm him right through. "Do you think perhaps it is time we dispense with the formality? You are closer to me at the moment than any other person, so I think Maria would be just fine."

"Very well, Maria," he said, enjoying the way her name sounded on his lips. "I would actually enjoy being called Hudson, I think, by someone other than my mother. Speaking of my mother — she is coming here."

Maria paused mid-chop, her mouth open, agape at his words. "Here? Your house?"

"Yes. Here."

"When?"

"Tonight."

"I see," she said, placing the knife down and turning around to face him, her hands curling around the counter behind her. "Would you like me to leave?"

"No," he said, overwhelmed for a moment by the intensity of the panic that gripped him at the thought of her going elsewhere, for fear that it would be the last he would ever see of her. He strode across the room until he stood in front of her, just shy from being able to reach out and stroke her cheek with the side of his finger. "In fact, I am thinking that perhaps it is time we inform her of your presence here."

Her eyes widened and she bit her lip, looking away from him and to the ground. "I-I thought you said she was nosy."

"She is," he admitted, "but she is not a gossip. She will ask questions, but she will keep your answers to herself."

"What if I do not wish to provide any answers?"

"Then don't."

Maria stood still for a moment, contemplating his words, until she finally let out a ragged sigh.

"Very well," she said. "If you trust her, then so do I. Should I set an extra plate for dinner?"

"She will likely bring something as well — she would never trust that I would have dinner prepared. If you also have a dish, we will be just fine."

Maria turned around, staring at what lay in front of her on the counter.

"Betsy began preparing a stew, but I told her I would finish. I need something to do. As you have come to know, I am not exactly the world's finest cook," she said with a short laugh. "I can chop and boil vegetables, but that is near the most of it."

"I do not suppose cooking is a skill learned by young ladies."

"Why, when there are useful skills such as dancing and watercolors to be perfected?" she asked, raising an eyebrow as she smiled, but there was no humor in her voice.

"Different people are raised to be proficient in different competencies," Hudson said carefully, stepping toward her and placing his hands on the bare skin of her upper arms before he even knew what he was doing, trapping her between his body and the counter.

"Yes, but most people have useful roles and professions. I am of no use to anyone."

"I would hardly say that."

She turned around, and suddenly her face was just below his, her pink, pert lips plush and kissable, her eyes a brilliant blue that seemed to see right into his soul.

He longed to lean down and taste her, but how could he, when he was the one man she seemed to trust?

"You may not know how to cook meat or darn socks or mop floors, but there is one thing you do know, and that is how to adapt to your circumstances, how to become better acquainted with people, how to move in a crowded room. These are important skills to have, no matter where you go in life. You also have such goodness in your heart and soul that are impossible to resist. You asked what you did to deserve help? You were yourself. Always. And that means a lot."

She began blinking rapidly as she looked away from him for a few moments, before finally turning her glistening eyes back to his.

"Thank you," she said softly. "I just worry about how I will look after myself."

A thought occurred to him then, one that should have struck him much earlier. He took a step back before her nearness, her scent of lemon and lavender, completely overwhelmed all of his senses.

"My mother assists me as I work. She calms families, makes notes for me, helps me with any tools I might need or speaks to the apothecary about particular medications. She is going to be away for a time. Why don't you assist me in her place?"

"Me?" Maria said, holding a hand up to her chest.

"Yes, you," he said with a teasing smile.

"Do you think that would be a wise idea?" she asked, scrunching up her nose. "I would be more than happy to do so, but I'm afraid that I might do something to endanger your business or insult one of your patients. I would have no idea what I am doing and—"

Hudson held up a finger to halt her flow of words.

"It was just a thought. You have no obligation to do so. I simply figured it would prove to you that you have a great amount of skill that could help many people — including me. And I would pay you for it, if you are looking to earn money."

She held up a hand at that, already shaking her head. "You will not pay me."

"But—"

"No!" she exclaimed now. "I would never take payment from you. However, I would consider doing this to show you how much your generosity has meant to me."

Hudson opened his mouth to argue, but at the earnestness in her gaze, the truth struck him, hard, deep in his chest. She needed this. She needed to feel that she was doing something to contribute, rather than having everything done for her.

If she could succeed here, then maybe she would gain confidence to create a life for herself, one that she would choose rather than would be chosen for her.

Although the thought of her going anywhere on her own was enough to make him want to reach out and hold her near and never let her go.

There was a knock on the door, and Maria's eyes widened in shock as she looked down at herself. Hudson managed a small smile of what he hoped appeared to be reassurance for her.

"Not to worry. My mother does not stand on ceremony. You look fine."

She looked beautiful, actually, but he could hardly say that aloud.

"Thank you," she murmured, moving into the middle of

the room and standing with her hands clasped in front of her.

"Mother," Hudson said as she pushed the door open before he could cross the room to allow her in. He would have to talk to her about that once more — a man required a modicum of privacy, at least. "Do come in."

"I brought—" she stopped after taking a step into the room. "I didn't realize that you had company."

"Lady Maria, this is my mother, Mrs. Lewis," he said, knowing from his work with the nobility that he was to introduce the highest-ranking person in the room first. "Mother, this is Lady Maria."

"Lady Maria?" she asked in a tone that made it clear she was not as impressed with the title as most people would be. "What are you doing in my son's home?"

"Mother," Hudson said with some admonishment, "can you please be welcoming? Lady Maria has run from a... troubling situation. Smith found her injured and brought her to me. She had nowhere else to go."

"I see," his mother said, softening somewhat when she realized that Maria was there in some distress. "I apologize, Lady Maria. I have not had the best of experiences with the noble set."

"I understand," Maria said graciously, and Hudson had the feeling that one skill she had mastered was knowing the correct thing to say at the exact appropriate time.

"Your son has offered to be a most gracious host until my friend returns from her time away. I know that this is not the most ideal of circumstances for him, but I will be sure to repay him for his generosity."

"How... interesting," his mother said, and Hudson nearly rolled his eyes at her. It seemed that her initial suspicion was changing somewhat, as she was now looking back and forth from Maria to him with some interest in her eyes — interest that he knew far too well. Match-making interest.

"Mother, it is not a possibility," he said, shaking his head in warning.

Maria looked up at him, somewhat perplexed.

"I will explain later," he said, hoping that she would actually forget this conversation entirely.

"What exactly are you running from?" his mother asked, as direct as ever, walking through the house and to the back room, Maria taking a few short steps behind her so that she was within speaking distance. Hudson was inclined to tell her that she was actually better off staying farther away, but he knew she was far too polite to do so.

"It is difficult to talk about but… a troubling marriage."

"Ah," his mother said, her face taking on sympathy. "That is an impossible position for a woman. I admire your bravery for leaving."

"Thank you," Maria said with some surprise. "But I truly don't think it was brave at all. I should have stayed and tried to change things. Should have tried to fix—"

His mother shocked him now by leaving the food on the counter and walking toward Maria. She reached out and took her hands.

"In many situations, particularly such as those you are describing, there is no fixing. There is only knowing when you should walk away." She looked back at Hudson now, who found himself an observer of the scene in front of him. "My son is a good man. And an excellent physician. I saw you limping earlier. Was it your ankle?"

"My ankle, yes. I also sustained a head injury, but I think, overall, I am doing much better."

She looked at Hudson for confirmation, and he nodded. "She has been a most exemplary patient. She rests when I tell her and does not overexert herself."

39

"I suppose an understanding of rest is one benefit of being part of the nobility," his mother muttered. While there was no malice in her tone, he did shoot her a look of warning.

"I have suggested that Maria assist me while you are away, Mother."

His mother seemed startled by that, but Maria quickly stepped in.

"Where are you going? A holiday sounds lovely."

"Bath."

"Oh, Bath, how beautiful! Have you been before?"

"No," his mother said with a laugh, returning to the food and beginning to fix it onto three plates. "It has not been possible for a woman such as me until now. I am greatly looking forward to it."

"It is lovely," Maria said, and as his mother began asking questions, they fell into easy conversation that made Hudson breathe a sigh of relief.

His desire for Maria had been apparent from the first day he had met her. Now, the warmth that filled him at seeing her get on well with his mother made him realize that Maria was becoming one of the most important women in his life.

Which worried him more than the thought of them meeting ever possibly had.

CHAPTER 6

aria squared her shoulders and did what she always did when she was walking into a situation she felt much anticipation for — she imagined, for that moment, that she was someone else.

Although this time, instead of pretending that she was the Diamond of the First Water that all of the men wanted and all of the women wanted to be, she imagined something much sweeter, something that she could never admit for it could never actually come into being — that she was the wife of Hudson Lewis, ready to spend the day with him as she assisted him in his house calls.

She could not even put into words how preferable that would be to her reality.

She closed her eyes as she tried to forget what she had seen yesterday. She hadn't meant to invade his privacy. At least, not at first. She knew that when she walked by the bedroom door, which had opened a crack — it never latched properly, she had learned — she should have continued walking instead of stopping and taking her time to determine just what she was seeing through the crack.

But she had known. And she had wanted to see more. It was Hudson, shirtless, as he changed into his clothing for the day. Then he had started to unfasten his breeches, and she had stood, mesmerized by the sight of him — until he began to turn toward where she stood at the door, and she had scurried away as fast as her injuries allowed her before he could possibly discover her.

Now, knowing what he looked like, how his strong, sinewy muscle tapered into sculpted abdominals with that trail of hair that led down below his breeches, she could hardly look him in the face.

She had spent the entirety of the short drive to his first patient with her head down staring at the sole horse pulling the gig in front of her, but luckily he had misinterpreted the implication.

"You have nothing to worry about," he had said with that helpful smile of his, one that she could see many a patient falling for. "You will be completely fine."

She hoped so. But when they stepped into the first house this morning, he was immediately taken to a back room without even a greeting, leaving Maria standing in the small foyer, alone, completely unsure of what to do.

Until she spied a little girl peering out from around the corner. Maria crouched with a smile, holding out a hand in invitation for the girl to come near, hoping she wouldn't appear too frightening.

After a few hesitant steps, the girl came running toward her, and Maria realized that maybe she could prove herself useful after all.

* * *

"That's all, then, Mr. Norley. I hope you have a pleasant day."

"Thank you, Dr. Lewis. And I must say, as much as I do enjoy your mother, the lovely young woman who accompanied you today cheered me up just by smiling at me."

Hudson laughed as he followed the hobbling man out of the back bedroom where Hudson had treated him, although he hoped he was right in thinking his patient's limp was slightly less pronounced than when he came in.

Hudson had told Maria that he would be just fine seeing to Mr. Norley without her help — and he stepped out of the room now to see how she was doing. He knew she would likely be bored waiting for him when he didn't need her assistance, yet somehow wherever they went, she seemed to find a way to make herself useful. And no matter where they were or who he was treating, he hadn't been able to take his mind off her all morning, knowing she was just on the other side of a wall.

Now, he saw that she was too busy for him. Unfortunately, they had been seen entering Mr. Norley's, and now she was standing just outside with Mrs. Bloomsbury — a woman who was far too gossipy for her own good, not that Maria would be aware of the woman's reputation. She must have knocked on the door to inquire who was within.

"Good day, Mrs. Bloomsbury," he said, joining them in front of the house. "How is that shoulder of yours?"

The woman let out a snort at that, before lifting her cane — one he knew she didn't need but carried for effect and stamped it purposefully on the ground.

"We shall see how long the latest lasts," she said, giving him one good long look as though to say she didn't trust him before turning back to Maria and continuing to speak. Hudson decided to give Maria a moment before he insisted on the urgency to continue on, and as he waited, an image across the cobblestone street caught his eyes.

A boy was holding a stack of newspapers in one hand,

waving one in the air to tempt passersby. "Morning Post!" he called out. "Learn all about the missing countess!"

Maria's head whipped around at that as she followed Hudson's gaze, both of them fixated by the sight. For there, on the front of the paper, was a likeness of her sketched upon it with the word "MISSING" written on top.

"Oh, goodness," she whispered, and before Hudson could stop her, she made a quick excuse to the suddenly speechless Mrs. Bloomsbury and was hurrying across the street, taking the paper right out of the boy's hand. Hudson followed behind, counting out a dear seven pence, knowing Maria likely didn't know how much the paper even cost, before taking her by the elbow and guiding her over to stand beside the brick wall of a building, out of the way of passersby.

"This would be you?" he asked, and she nodded woodenly, her eyes glued to the page.

"Maria," he said softly, placing an index finger beneath her chin and tilting her head up so that she was looking him in the eyes, "would you like me to read the article, or do you think perhaps it is time that you told me your story so perhaps I can do more to help you?"

She bit her lip, a sheen of tears covering them before she took a breath and nodded her head.

"Yes, I do think it's time."

"Let's go home, then," he said, enjoying the feeling when she placed her arm upon his. It felt right, like it belonged there — like *she* belonged here — even though he knew in his heart she belonged anywhere but.

* * *

MARIA KNEW that if she was safe with anyone, it was here, with Hudson.

But she was worried.

Worried that he would think less of her, that he would wonder why she had been so gullible, so stupid to allow herself to marry such a man as her now-husband, to not have prevented this situation before it had come to this point.

If only she had run away before she had been married. Then perhaps her situation living here with Hudson would be much different — although, knowing him, he would never allow her reputation as a single woman to come into question by staying with him. Perhaps he would have returned her home and she would have been back to where she had started.

He leaned over now, taking one of her hands in his in that way he had that was both comforting as well as curious in the desire it elicited within her, as she could so easily imagine those hands moving up her arms, over her shoulders, and down—no. She couldn't think like that. It wasn't right.

It also completely befuddled her that one touch from her husband had made her wish to run as far as she could in the other direction, while when Hudson's skin touched hers, she only wanted to pull him closer.

She took a breath, summoning her courage before looking up and meeting his eye as he sat waiting patiently for her to begin, not pressuring her, not asking questions, but simply giving her time to tell her story.

"You know I was married not long ago," she began.

"I do."

Was it her imagination, or was his voice a little growly?

"I didn't know him well. My parents had arranged the match after the duke — your half-brother — decided to marry Lady Emma instead of me. Which I understood. They were in love. But society didn't quite see it that way. They assumed there was something lacking with me, that perhaps I wasn't the prize they had all thought I was."

She heard the wryness in her tone but couldn't help it. She held nothing against the duke himself but couldn't help her annoyance that society would change all opinion held toward her based on a decision made by one man — a decision that had nothing to do with her but everything to do with the woman he had fallen in love with.

"The earl began to court me as expected, although we had limited time together. He was polite, the gentleman that he was supposed to be, although I always felt there was something… off about him. I questioned my reaction, however, as I could not quite determine what it was and he never acted in a manner that should have raised my suspicions." She laughed humorlessly. "I didn't trust myself. I listened to everyone else instead."

"You cannot blame yourself," he murmured, and she shrugged, staring off into the distance, to the corner of the room that felt more like home than her parent's country estate or London manor ever had.

"We married. Even as I said yes, I knew it was the wrong decision but what was I to do? I didn't have the courage to stand up for myself and say no in front of all who had gathered, to accept what would be sure ruin for both me and my family. It did not take long for him to show who he truly was after that. In fact, he did so moments later, in the carriage. Fortunately, the drive was too short for… for anything to occur."

She swallowed hard as she shivered at the remembrance of that brief encounter with him. What would a lifetime with the man bring?

"After the wedding breakfast, my lady's maid, Anne, brought another maid to see me. She told me the truth of it all — that he had been torturing the poor maids for years. That not only did he force himself upon them, but he had done so in a cr-cruel manner."

She clapped a hand over her mouth as the reality of who the man truly was and what he had been doing for so long hit her with full force.

"She came to warn me to reveal my pain early on as he does not stop until he achieves his aim."

At that the tears began to run down her face, and Hudson moved from the chair across from her to sit next to her on the sofa. He hesitated, as though unsure of how close he should come, but she nodded her agreement and he seemed to understand as he placed an arm around her shoulders and drew her close. She took the comfort he offered and leaned into him.

When she spoke again, her voice was just above a whisper, but now that she had started, she had to see the story through.

"He came to me that night. He had a r-riding crop. He told me what he was going to do, but he had to go relieve himself first. Then, finally, I acted. I did not even think. I just went out the window and down the trellis. When I reached the bottom, I heard him shout from above and that's when my ankle turned. My resolve, however, was greater than the pain I felt, and I made it to the edge of Mayfair with the help of a fallen tree branch to lean upon. I was able to find a ride — from a family kind enough to take pity on me and not ask any questions — to the edge of Holborn. I was trying to find Juliana but became horribly lost. I was confused, I was hurt, I —that's when I must have fallen into the building. Thank goodness the man who found me was trustworthy and brought me to you. It could have been—"

She shook her head then, unable to finish. What had begun as the most horrible night of her life could have ended even worse.

Hudson wrapped his arms around her then, pulling her in and holding her close. Her hands rose to circle his neck and she accepted the embrace, drawing strength from his hard frame against her and the solace he provided.

"I cannot go back," she choked out, crying into the rough material of his jacket at his shoulder, and he shook his head rapidly.

"You absolutely cannot." He gripped her harder, one hand stroking over her hair. She heard a pin drop from it, but she didn't care. "Whatever you need, Maria, I will give it to you if it will keep you safe. I promise you that. He will not hurt you — no one will. I will not allow it."

He said it so fiercely, that for a moment, Maria held out hope that she was no longer alone.

"But... why?" she asked into his shoulder.

"You know why," he said, even as she shook her head. She was married. It could never be. *They* could never be, as much as they both wished it to be so.

"Oh, Hudson," she said, squeezing her arms around his neck before lifting her head up to look at him. Their lips were but a breath away from one another's, but he didn't move — which she knew was due to the story she had told, and his respect for her after how her husband had threatened her.

She shifted ever so slightly, so that their lips were just touching, and her invitation seemed to be enough as he let out a true growl and his lips began to move over hers — though slowly, with some hesitation. He stopped before she could truly begin enjoying the kiss, leaning back from her and whispering against her lips, "Is this all right?"

She nodded and leaned up to accept him again. She had no idea what she was doing — she had never kissed before — but their lips seemed to already know one another and how to respond without her even having to think about it. The kiss was gentle yet passionate, an outpouring of all they had held within.

Maria was married. She knew that. Yet her connection with Hudson seemed far truer than anything she had with her husband, vows or not.

Finally, they broke away, though Hudson rested his forehead against hers as they breathed the same air, for they seemingly were unable to move away from one another.

"Oh, Maria," he said, his fingers toying with the back of her neck, but his voice drifted off, for she knew there was so much to say but yet it was too difficult for either of them to put into words.

"What are we going to do?" she asked. "I know I am safe, but… the maids. How can I protect them? I need to make sure that Anne — my lady's maid — was able to return to my parents, and I promised Jane, the one who came to me, that I would help her find another position, to get away. How can I do that, when I have run away like a coward?"

"You are no coward," he said, his thumb stroking her cheek. "You are far braver than you know. We need help," he said with conviction. "And fortunately, I believe Archibald and Juliana were to return today. They can be trusted."

"They can," she agreed, even as a part of her was slightly saddened at the thought she no longer had any reason to stay with Hudson. The idea that she must part with him was nearly more than she could bear.

"There's something else," she said. "Jane claimed that she believes one of the maids might have…" she swallowed hard, "…might have died at his hand. The staff was told she left of her own will, but no one ever heard of her again. This is not a world in which he would be tried for the death of a maid, but—"

"But we can try," he finished, conviction in his tone. "We will go to Matthew tomorrow. Until then, you should get some sleep."

She nodded, standing and walking back to the bedroom.

She stopped in the doorway, looking back to watch him begin to arrange his blankets in front of the fire on the sofa for the night.

"Hudson?"

"Yes?"

"Would you... would you sleep with me tonight? Not to... that is... would you hold me?"

"Of course," he said, and she couldn't help her heart from picking up its beat as he followed her into the bedroom.

CHAPTER 7

*H*udson couldn't have said no to her request —
but saying yes was certainly more dangerous.

He was still shaking after hearing her story. He had
masked his true emotion so as not to scare her once more,
but he had been seething with rage. He knew there were
many men like her husband in the world, of course — he had
seen plenty of evidence of their actions with his own eyes —
but to think of what Maria's life could have been had she
stayed... he only wished that he had known sooner, that he
could have helped her, stopped the wedding before it had
ever occurred.

But that was foolish. For how was he ever to have known
when he had been doing all he could to stay away from her,
to not even think of her?

He most certainly shouldn't have kissed her. But he
hadn't been able to help his need to claim her, to show her
that not every man was like her husband, that his own feelings for her were of another sort entirely.

He paused in the doorway when she stopped by the bed,

her hands twining together as she stared at him with some uncertainty, as though she was already regretting asking him.

"I'll wait out here to give you a moment to ready yourself," he said, and she nodded gratefully.

Hudson closed the door, taking deep breaths to try to calm the storm within him. The angry turmoil from her story mixed with the desire that being around her arose in his body, no matter how hard he told himself he had to tamp it down.

There was no room for that tonight, however. That was not why she needed him, not what she was looking for — she was running from it, in fact.

"I-I'm ready," she called from within, and he opened the door before walking over, sitting on the edge of the bed and pulling off his boots, doing all he could not to scare her or to remind her of what she had been through.

He had brought his blanket with him and unfolded it on top of the one she lay under.

"Will you be warm enough?" she asked, and he was touched that she would think of his own comfort.

"Of course," he said. He would be more than warm with her sleeping beside him.

He lay next to her gently, leaving space between them, allowing her to tell him what she needed.

"Hudson?" she asked, her voice small in the darkness.

"Yes?"

"Would you talk to me, tell me more about you?"

Hudson would spend all night talking to her, but he wasn't entirely sure what he was supposed to say, nor what she would think of the life he had lived.

"There isn't much to tell, really."

"Where did you grow up? What was your childhood like?"

He was silent for a moment as he thought back on it, wondering how much to tell her, finally deciding that she had shared the entirety of her story with him, so how could he not trust her in the same manner?

"I grew up in the village of Watford. My mother had worked for the Remington family as a maid at Remington House, where the duke took an interest in her."

Maria was silent as she listened to his story, but he could tell by the nature of her breathing that she was still awake.

"She was not averse to his attentions, but she didn't realize his true nature until it was too late. He was newly married but had told her stories of how cold his wife was. It was likely true that the duchess was not interested in being near him, but it just wasn't apparent why until later."

"I can understand that."

"My mother went to the duke when she found out she was with child, and he told her to pack her things and leave. His wife didn't know at the time. All my mother asked for was money to support me. The duke refused, so she told his wife about the babe. She also told him she would continue to inform all of society unless he began the payments. She moved into the village and fabricated a story about being married to a soldier who died in battle. Since she seemed to have money to live, they believed her. She made some money herself as a seamstress, although she was not particularly talented."

"She is a strong woman."

"She is. She was insistent that I would live the life of a gentleman, and ensured that when the time came, I was educated to become a physician. That was when we moved to London and began our life here."

"Was your childhood happy?"

"It was. Some people had an inkling of the true story and would call me bastard now and again, but for the most part the life I knew was enjoyable."

"Did you always want to be a physician?"

"I never considered anything else," he said, although as he said it, he knew he was happy with the life he had in front of him.

"Is there... anything else you wanted out of life?"

He nodded, and then when he realized she couldn't see him, he continued. "Yes. A family. A wife. Children of my own, who would be born with my name, not a bastard like me."

She stilled slightly at that, and he knew it hadn't been the right thing to say, although it was the truth.

"Would you hold me?" she asked again, her voice just above a whisper, and Hudson had never been more grateful to answer a request in his life.

"Of course," he said before shifting closer, wrapping his arm around her, holding her back to his front. He angled his hips backward so she wouldn't feel the evidence of his desire for her, evidence that he was doing his very best to talk down.

She was tense at first, but eventually her breathing slowed and she relaxed into him, falling asleep.

Whether Hudson would ever do the same was another story.

* * *

WHEN MARIA AWOKE the next morning, she felt more rested than she had in weeks — ever since she'd discovered she was going to be married, in fact. Hudson was already out of bed, and she could hear him outside the room, likely preparing tea for the two of them as he always did.

Maria couldn't help the small smile that crossed her face when she thought of his closeness last night, of how supportive he had been. He was unlike any man she had ever met before, and she wished she had taken a chance on him much earlier — before it was too late.

Today was the one day a week Hudson did not schedule any rounds, which made it the perfect opportunity to visit Juliana and Matthew.

"Should I pack my few belongings? Or do I leave them here to return to where you found them?"

Hudson shook his head. "They were gifts," he said, and she had a sneaking suspicion he had purchased them for her, although he had never admitted it to her. "But I suppose you can leave them here until we determine what our next steps are."

Our next steps. Maria wasn't sure why it meant so much to her that he had taken on her plight as his own, but as much as she felt like she should tell him she was fine, she couldn't help but appreciate it — appreciate *him*.

Hudson kept a hand on her back as he helped her up into his gig before driving through the winding streets of Holborn. Maria's back tingled where he had touched her, and even now she could feel the warmth of his shoulder against hers through the material of her dress until they came to Juliana and Matthew's house.

"I was a fool to think I could find this on my own in the dark," she murmured as Hudson knocked on the door before shaking his head.

"Far better than the alternative."

"True."

The door flew open to reveal Juliana standing there. Her friendly face froze into one of shock before she launched herself out the door, throwing her arms around Maria.

"Oh, Maria, I am so glad to see you! We were so worried."

Tears sprang anew in Maria's eyes that she had a friend who would care so deeply about her, and she returned the genuine embrace that she was not used to receiving in her previous circles.

"We heard you were missing and that your family was looking for you. Oh, Maria, I feared— I feared the worst."

"You knew about her husband, then?" Hudson asked from behind her, an edge to his voice, and Juliana started, as though just realizing her half-brother was there.

"Hudson!" she exclaimed. "What are you—never mind that. Come in and we will all discuss this further."

She opened the door wider to welcome them in, her husband, Matthew Archibald, appearing behind her as she did so. Before Maria could say anything, animals came surging toward the door — dogs and cats, and... was that a bird flying toward her? She let out a little gasp as she ducked, but when she looked up, Juliana and her husband seemed unbothered.

"Our apologies. They are all friendly I assure you. Lewis. Lady Maria—that is Lady Dennison," Mr. Archibald greeted them, his face devoid of his true reaction, as it always was. Maria allowed the little dog to lick her hand as she took it all in.

"Please call me Maria, Mr. Archibald," she said, never wanting to be referred to as Lady Dennison again.

"Very well. Matthew it is, then," he said. "Please come in."

As Maria walked past him into the small foyer, she could hear him say, "I suppose I should have taken that job after all. This would have been the easiest case I have ever solved."

Maria whirled around, shaking her head frantically.

"You cannot tell anyone I am here. No one," she said, looking from Juliana to Matthew with supplication, and Juliana reached out and placed a hand on her arm.

"I know. And we won't. I told Matthew that we had to be very careful with this case and he turned down your husband

and your father this very morning upon our return. But come, let's sit. Would you like tea?"

"No, thank you," Maria said, sitting down on the sofa as one of the dogs curled up at her feet. She was grateful when Hudson took the seat next to her.

"Are you injured? Ill? How did you come to find Hudson?" Juliana asked before she had even poured tea, and her husband sat next to her and placed a hand on her leg.

"Why do we not let Lady Maria tell us what brings her here, love?" he asked, and Juliana nodded.

"Of course. I apologize. When we returned and found that you were missing, I was terrified. Matthew was just readying himself to begin searching for you when you arrived."

Maria took a breath. "I am sorry to have worried you. When I… left, I actually came to Holborn to seek you out. I had some trouble finding you, I suppose you could say." She paused, wondering how much to tell them, then decided that if she wanted their help, she would have to tell them all.

"I should have known not to marry him," she began, before recounting to them what had happened in the carriage as soon as they had left the church, then continuing on to what Jane had told her and finally what had happened when her husband had entered her room. She omitted a few of the more sordid details, but even so, her face was flushed with heat telling the story with Juliana's husband present. Maria had been raised to never utter an inappropriate word in the company of a man — or any polite company at all — but somehow telling Hudson hadn't seemed like the breaking of that rule. She wasn't sure if it was because he was a physician or because she trusted him.

Mr. Archibald was a detective, so Maria continued to remind herself that he was likely used to such stories, though it didn't seem to help much. She stumbled in her storytelling, which was punctuated by Juliana's gasps and outbursts of anger, but she finally made it to the end.

"Oh, Maria," Juliana said, reaching a hand across the table and taking Maria's in hers. "I am so sorry for all that happened to you."

"There is nothing to be sorry for," Maria said grimly. "I allowed the wedding to happen, and I was fortunate enough to escape before anything... untoward occurred. Which is not the same that I can say for some of the poor girls that I left behind."

She paused, ignoring Juliana's insistence that she had done nothing wrong in escaping.

"Actually," Maria continued, setting her shoulders back, "that is why I'm here. Something must be done. That man cannot continue to traumatize all the innocent girls that come into his employ. There was even talk amongst the maids that he... that he went too far with one, that perhaps she did not simply go missing."

Juliana made a sound of disgust before sitting up straight with determination. "Of course we will help," she said enthusiastically, but her husband stopped her by holding up a hand.

"We do want to do all that we can to help you," he said. "But we must consider what is possible. The man is a highly regarded earl. No one will believe — or at least, act upon — the allegations of a few maids. I hate to say it, but no one would act upon accusations from any woman. And you are his wife, so..."

"I belong to him. He can do as he pleases," Maria said in a small voice.

"In the eyes of the law," he said, before letting out a sigh, for he obviously knew his words wouldn't be welcomed, "yes."

"Isn't there anything else we can do?" Juliana asked, her

eyes boring into Matthew's, and he reached out and took her hand in his.

"Let me think about it," he said before turning to Maria. "Perhaps there is a way to threaten his reputation, to cause him to consider his behavior in the future. In the meantime, Lad—Maria, what do you plan to do?"

"I…" Maria looked over at Hudson, waiting for him to say something, but he remained silent. "I was hoping to ask if I could stay here, now that you are returned." She looked around, for she had never been in here before. Their home was not overly big, but she supposed she could make do with the sofa, although she wasn't certain which creatures she would be sleeping with.

"If that is what you wish, of course you can stay here," Juliana said. "We do not have an additional bed at the moment, but Matthew could sleep in front of the fire, and you could—"

"Oh, no, I could not put you out like that," Maria said, immediately shaking her head. She looked to Hudson, hesitant in asking even more from him, but he smoothly interjected before she could say anything.

"You can continue to stay with me," he said. "I do not mind sleeping in front of the hearth so much."

"But—"

"My only concern is what it could mean regarding your reputation," he said, to which she shrugged.

"That is already gone."

"Very well," he said, before looking up to meet his half-sister's eyes. Hers were flitting back and forth between them, obviously assessing there was more here than a simple friendship, although she fortunately didn't comment upon it.

"There's something else," Maria said suddenly. "Something just as important, that I should have mentioned before, as soon as we arrived."

"We have time," Matthew said calmly.

"I wasn't in my husband's company long, but on two occasions I heard him mention the Duke of Warwick — not your brother, Juliana, but your father."

"In what regard?" Matthew said, leaning forward as both Juliana and Hudson wore looks of surprise at the news. She should have mentioned it to Hudson before but hadn't been sure what his feelings were on the man he had recently discovered was his father.

"Once he did not know I could hear him. We were on a drive, and he was speaking with another lord about how fortunate he was that the duke had perished, that it caused him a great deal of relief. Then, when we were deciding who to invite to the wedding, I had requested to add you, Juliana, and his mother made a comment to him about your family — that he was now finally free of you and it would best if it were to remain that way. I am not sure if that is particularly helpful. Had I stayed, perhaps I could have discovered more."

"You most certainly should *not* have stayed," Juliana said, her gaze piercing Maria's.

Matthew's voice cut through as he stood between them. "Lewis and I should give the two of you a moment alone. Lewis, I have a small study at the back of the house. Join me there?"

Maria wondered just what they had to discuss that she and Juliana couldn't hear, but she didn't question it. She had asked for their help, and she would accept what they could provide.

Once they were gone, Juliana moved from her chair to take Hudson's seat, and she gathered Maria's hands in hers.

"Oh, Maria," she said, her eyes full of sympathy that Maria wished she didn't require. "What are you going to do now? What do you *want* to do?"

"I suppose I have to find a way to support myself while I

hide from the earl," she said. "I have no other recourse. Unfortunately, I do not have many useful skills. Hudson has allowed me to work with him while his mother is away, but I am not good for much besides entertaining young children and comforting husbands or wives."

"I am sure that is of a great assistance to him," Juliana said with a reassuring smile.

"It is only for a brief time, however," Maria said. "Then I shall have to find something else."

Juliana studied her for a moment.

"You will find the path forward, Maria," she said with conviction. "I am sure of it."

Maria wished she could hold the same certainty. How, she had no idea. For the truth was, she was glad this situation could not be permanent. Even for these short few days, she had no idea how she could continue to remain so close to Hudson, working with him through the day, sleeping under the same roof during the night, and keep herself from falling in love with him.

But what other choice did she possibly have but to resist?

CHAPTER 8

Their visit to Matthew and Juliana had given Hudson much to consider — the information Maria had held, how involved she was now in what potentially could have been a plot against his own father, and what it would all mean for her future.

If the earl suspected that Maria knew something about the duke's death and he was, in fact, involved, would it provide him an additional reason to search for her... and possibly ensure her continued silence?

They didn't speak much on their return home, and he wondered how she felt about remaining with him, for whatever amount of time they had left together.

But he would enjoy their time together while he could.

She continued to work with him, and as much as he focused on his patients, he enjoyed watching her work. Sometimes she would assist him in treating the patient, while other times she would talk to the patient's family, keeping them calm and providing him the space to work as he needed to.

From what he could tell, she was gaining confidence in

her role, and he hoped that she was beginning to realize her importance.

He told her that as much as he could, and he hoped she believed him.

In the meantime, her ankle had healed quickly and while she still suffered some occasional dizziness if she stood too quickly or worked for too long, she was feeling much better overall and her head wound had healed.

They were leaving a patient's home at the edge of Holborn when a young boy found him, breathing hard when he caught up to Hudson and Maria as they stepped away from the front door.

"Dr. Hudson!" he called out, and Hudson came to a stop.

"Yes, lad?"

"You're needed in Mayfair. A girl with fever that continues to worsen."

"How old is she?" Hudson asked, immediately beginning to determine as much as he could about the case. While most of his work was in Holborn, he was called to Mayfair from time to time. He'd had families request to hire him on as their physician, but despite the temptation of the salary, it hadn't felt like the right choice for him.

"I believe five and ten, Doctor."

"Thank you," he said, changing direction as he began toward his gig, stopping when he suddenly felt rather alone. He looked behind him to see Maria standing on the side of the street, all of the color drained from her face as she stared at him.

"Is something amiss?" he asked, and she finally blinked.

"I cannot go to Mayfair."

"Of course," he said, guilt rushing through him. He had completely forgotten her situation in his urgency to attend to the girl. "I will take you home first."

"Doctor?" the boy approached, appearing somewhat

apprehensive. "I hate to tell ya what to do, but she's in a bad way."

Maria took a breath and squared her shoulders in that way of hers that told him she was preparing herself to face something she'd prefer not to.

"I have a bonnet," she said. "I'll keep it low and not look anyone in the eye. I'm sure it will be fine."

"Maria, you cannot risk—"

"I will not risk a young girl's life over my fear of walking through Mayfair. We should go."

She began to move toward the gig as the boy gave a nod as though he approved of her decision, and Hudson found that he had no choice but to follow, as conflicted as he was.

Maria's step hitched ever so slightly as they neared Mayfair, but she set her jaw resolutely, until they came to a stop in front of a house that Hudson didn't recognize.

"Do you know the house?"

"No," she shook her head. "But I believe we are next door to Lord Hemingway's home. He is—"

"Cousin to the Duke of Warwick," Hudson finished for her. "Which makes him my cousin, in a sense, I suppose."

"I suppose," Maria agreed.

"Do you think it is best you come in or stay outside?"

"I'd better not enter in case it is a family who would recognize me. I will sit across the way near the square. There is a bench in the shadow of a tree where I can stay fairly inconspicuous."

"I should not leave you alone," Hudson hedged, uncertain what to do, panicking slightly at the thought that anyone could happen upon her and he would be helpless to do anything.

"I shall be fine," she said. "If anything happens, I will call out. The house is right there. Now hurry to your patient."

"Very well," he said. "I shall be as quick as possible."

And he walked into the house, feeling as though he was leaving something very important behind.

* * *

MARIA SAT BACK into the depths of the bench, hoping her face would be hidden by the shadows and her bonnet. Surely no one would guess that the woman in the somewhat lovely though rather rough-hewn clothes was Lady Maria Dennison. Quite a few minutes passed by before an elderly woman sat next to her on the bench, and Maria stiffened, keeping her gaze forward, hoping she would not attempt conversation.

"Many people are looking for you, you know."

Maria started, unable to help herself from turning to see who had spoken to her. Her mouth dropped open to find none other than Lady Winchester, grandmother to Juliana and her siblings, sitting next to her.

"Lady Winchester," Maria said before looking around furtively to see if she was accompanied by anyone, "I—that is, how did you know I was here?"

"I was walking by and happened to notice you. I am more observant than most."

"I see," Maria said, her heart picking up its pace as she looked to the door to see if Hudson was going to emerge soon. She knew that with these types of ailments, it could either be quick and straightforward, or it could take some time to assess what could be causing the fever. "I am not supposed to be in Mayfair, Lady Winchester. A… situation brought me here, but I will be leaving again very soon. I know this is an odd request, but if you could keep from telling anyone I am here, I would be ever so grateful."

"Not to worry, Lady Maria," Lady Winchester said, and Maria appreciated that somehow she knew Maria wouldn't appreciate the use of her new title. "Your secret is safe with me. I do, however, have one question that has been nagging at me."

"Yes?"

"Why did you marry the man in the first place?"

Maria looked down.

"I had no choice. My parents arranged it—"

"And most women would follow through with it, that I understand," Lady Winchester said. "But *most* women also wouldn't run when they realized what they had gotten themselves into."

"It was rather cowardly of me, wasn't it?"

"Cowardly?" Lady Winchester scoffed, stomping her cane on the ground, and Maria thought that the woman would perhaps get on rather well with Mrs. Bloomsbury. "I say it was brave."

"Thank you, Lady Winchester," Lady Maria said, wondering where the woman was going with this.

"Your husband and your father are on the hunt for you," Lady Winchester said in a low voice. "I suspect for your husband it is a matter of pride, and while your parents are worried about you, they would have to ensure you were returned to the man. I will not say a word, but Lady Maria, the story is everywhere, as you can imagine. I cannot see any way out of this for you, except for you to leave London."

"Leave London?" Maria asked, her mouth gaping wide. She had never considered that before. It was an obvious choice, she realized now, but she knew nothing about any other country — she hardly knew anywhere besides London. Even when they visited her family's country estate, they hardly ventured off the property except for church service. Where would she go? What would she do?

"You're best to go to America, if you can," Lady Winchester said as though reading her thoughts. "If not, at least to the country somewhere. Take a position as a governess or something of the like."

Maria's mouth gaped open. America?

"A governess? I would have no idea—"

"You best learn, then," Lady Winchester said resolutely, and for a moment, Maria wished she could be more like this woman, with the resolution to do anything necessary to achieve her aim. "If you need help, I will do what I can for you."

She leaned on her cane to stand.

"Well, I best go join my daughter. I told her I was going to enjoy the rare sunshine for a time before I joined her within as she called on Lady Hemingway. Truth is, the less time I can spend in that mausoleum of a place, the better. Good day, Lady Maria. I wish I could say that I look forward to seeing you again, but I think it is best we both wish that will not occur."

With that, she walked away, shortly before Hudson emerged from the house, looking one way and the next for her, his shoulders dropping in relief when he saw her, and he rushed across to the square.

"Maria, thank goodness," he said.

"Is all well?"

"The girl should be fine, I hope," he said. "I've sent them on to the apothecary and hopefully if they continue to follow the measures I've instructed, the fever will break shortly. Did you see anyone? Were you recognized?"

"I did and I was," she said as he helped her into the gig once the servant brought it around. "By Lady Winchester."

He stopped still. "Lady Winchester?"

Maria nodded. "Hudson, she suggested that the best recourse for me is to leave London, likely for America. I feel a fool that I had never thought of such a thing but perhaps — perhaps she is right. That may be the only option I have. I shall feel as though I am running away, but what else is there for me to do?"

He was silent for a moment, his gaze ahead of him.

Finally, he spoke. "Archibald said that your maid, Anne, is safe and returned to your family's employ. He promised he would see what he could do in determining where Jane is and finding her employment elsewhere. I know you are concerned for any other maids who are hired by the family, or any other young women who come into the earl's path, but I do not see how we can possibly address such a thing. Perhaps you could ask Lady Winchester — or even Lady Prudence — to provide a reference for Jane, seeing as though you can hardly do so yourself anymore. I'm sure you would feel better once she is looked after, would you not?"

"You're right," Maria said, a bit relieved that she had an excuse to stay. "And I would also like to help in determining what Lord Dennison had to do with the former Duke of Warwick."

Hudson's face darkened slightly at that. "Do you not think it best to stay out of that? I do not like the thought of you becoming involved. One man has been murdered and an entire family threatened."

"I would like to help if I can," she said, setting her jaw in determination. "Juliana has become a good friend of mine, and I would never want to see her in danger again."

Hudson nodded. "I know how terrifying it was for everyone when Juliana was abducted," he said. "I shouldn't like her or anyone else to be under threat, but I know that will be the case until whoever is terrorizing the family is caught or they succeed in killing the duke, which I know must be prevented."

Maria nodded. The threats to the family had made it clear that the former duke had been murdered, and Matthew had been hired to investigate and keep the family safe. In the process he had fallen in love with Juliana and she with him. Maria knew that Matthew had despaired of the fact that he had not yet solved this case — each avenue led nowhere.

"We will have to be careful," Hudson said. "But we will make it work."

They had returned to Holborn and were close to his residence when a man who Maria recognized as Smith approached. Hudson pulled on the reins to slow his horse.

"Doc, would you come take a quick look at my daughter?" he asked, and Hudson looked over at Maria, who nodded. Of course they would go. The rest could wait.

This time when Hudson treated the patient, Maria stayed in the room and assisted, as it was a broken finger that he felt he could set himself without having to call the surgeon. He was so kind, so compassionate, that a couple of times Maria stopped what she was doing to simply watch him.

As she did, she realized that her fears had become founded, but that it was too late to do anything to put a stop to what was happening. She was falling hopelessly in love with Hudson.

CHAPTER 9

"Maria?"

Hudson had been called to a patient in Mayfair that morning, and this time Maria had stayed home in order to avoid any potential encounters with someone she might know.

"Yes?" she said, coming out of the bedroom, where she had been determining which of her clothing needed cleaning. She actually wasn't certain just what to do with the garments, for she normally simply gave them to Anne. There was a chance Hudson's maid could help but decided she would ask Juliana. Surely she would know.

"I received a note from Archibald."

"Oh?"

"He wants to meet with us at his home. But not just with him and Juliana. He feels that all of the siblings should be there."

Maria's heart started to beat a little faster at the thought. It was one thing to share all with Hudson, or even Juliana and Matthew, but Lady Prudence? The Duke and Duchess of Warwick? It would be rather humiliating.

"They already know your circumstances," he said quietly, apparently understanding her concerns, "and they only want to help, as well as learn a bit more about Lord Dennison and his connection to their father."

"Very well," she said, then took a deep breath. She had said she wanted to assist them in turn, and if this was the way forward, then so be it. "If they can help with Jane and if I can offer any information that might provide a clue as to who is threatening them, then we shall go. But I have already told Matthew all that I know."

"He is hoping you know more than you realize," Hudson said.

"When are we meeting?"

"This evening if you do not oppose."

"Best get it over with."

"That's the spirit," he said with a slight chuckle.

And so, a few hours later they were once more walking up to Juliana and Matthew's door. Hudson already knew to give Maria a moment to collect herself before continuing in.

He wasn't sure that she even realized she always took those few seconds to prepare herself before entering, and he wondered anew just what was going through her head when she did so.

"Come in," Juliana said with a welcoming smile as she opened the door and took Maria's elbow in hers, inter-locking their arms in a gesture that Hudson assumed was to provide support. This time, both he and Maria were prepared and braced themselves to accept the animal welcome.

Juliana led them into the small drawing room, where most of the furniture was covered in Remingtons and cats. The Duke of Warwick was there with his wife, who Hudson knew had been close friends with Juliana before marrying into the family. Juliana and Archibald were present of course, and then there was Lady Prudence, the duke and Juliana's sister — Hudson's own half-sister. She looked like Juliana, with chestnut hair and green eyes resembling their mother, while Hudson was aware that he and the duke shared the look of their father. He was surprised to see that Lady Winchester had joined them, although her daughter and the siblings' mother, the dowager duchess, was not present.

"Good evening," the duke said in his deep voice with a nod and what Hudson thought was, perhaps, actually a contrite look sent his way. The duke had apologized — as much as a duke ever would — for his assumptions of Hudson's guilt, but he hadn't been able to take back the accusations. "Thank you for coming."

"I am happy to do all I can to help," said Maria as she took a seat in one of the two remaining chairs. "Before we begin, I do want to thank you all for keeping my whereabouts secret."

"It is a rather shocking situation, isn't it?" Lady Prudence said. "But then, we are no longer shocked by much in this family."

Her comment caused some of the tension to leave the room, and Archibald stood, as he had obviously been the one who thought it be best that they all meet together.

"Since you mentioned it, Lady Maria, let us begin there," he said. "After our conversation, I had my men ask some discreet questions regarding Lord Dennison's household. He is currently most preoccupied with upholding his reputation, and he is concerned for the continuation of his line, of course. I have heard rumblings—" he shared a quick look with Juliana, who squeezed Maria's hand "—that at this point he feels it would best if you were to be declared dead, for then he could find, as he puts it, a much more 'willing wife.'"

Maria's breath left her lungs at both the thought of her apparent death and another woman suffering the fate she had previously avoided, but she waited for Matthew to continue.

"You must be very, very careful, Lady Maria, that he does not discover your whereabouts now. For if he does, I am afraid that he might attempt to put his words into action."

"Do you actually think he would go that far?" Lady Prudence asked with wide eyes.

Maria was the one to answer her, even though her voice shook slightly.

"According to the maids, he has killed before, although it would have been a crime of passion, I suppose you could say."

"Which means," Juliana said from beside her, "that he would also be capable of killing our father, or attempting to kill Giles, if he had a reason to do so."

"That is exactly the question," the duke said from where he sat in the chair across the room. "What reason would he have? Archibald said you believed he was angry with our father, Lady Maria, but would that be reason enough to kill him? And why come after me next?"

Maria shrugged her delicate shoulders. "I wish I knew. I only know that he was pleased your father had passed, that he said it made his life much easier. If only I had more information for you. Perhaps... the servants seemed quite sympathetic toward me. I could return to the servants' entrance in disguise and ask more information or find Jane. She might tell me—"

"No."

They all turned to Hudson, who was still standing across the room, staring at her. "Absolutely not. It is far too dangerous. Yes, there would be servants who would stand with you, but others will be loyal to their employer. If he discovered that you were not only nearby but also asking questions

73

ELLIE ST. CLAIR

about him and his connection to the Duke of Warwick, I shudder to think of how he might react."

The thought had him near to shaking in rage again, and when he saw Maria ball her hands into fists at her side, he knew she was similarly affected by her inability to do anything to help herself or this family.

"My men will be following up with Jane regardless," Matthew said, holding up a hand. "When we speak to her, we will determine if she knows anything else."

"She might be frightened, and I am not sure that she would tell a stranger anything," Maria said, to which Matthew nodded.

"We will ensure she knows that we are there on your behalf," he said. "It is all we can do. Lewis is right in that you cannot risk returning to the house."

"Wouldn't it be a wonderful situation if the earl turned out to be the killer?" Lady Prudence mused from her chair. "He could be charged and hanged and then we could all go back to living without fear for our lives."

"Prudence!" Juliana admonished, although there was not much conviction in her tone.

"Except that he could get off and then I would still be Lady Dennison," Maria said wryly, and Prudence inclined her head at that point.

"True. What if we faked Maria's death and framed Lord Dennison as the killer?" she asked, and they all went silent as they mulled over it.

"It could work," the duke finally said. "But we would need not only a body but also likely a witness for the House of Lords to ever even consider trying Dennison. I do not believe even Archibald would have the resources to bring it to fruition."

"We could try," Archibald said. "But it would be a gruesome business that has little chance of working."

"Very well," Hudson said. "We will find another way forward."

"Does anyone have any idea why Lord Dennison might have taken issue with Father?" Juliana asked.

The duke scoffed. "We could list multitudes of reasons. He could have been in debt to him. Father could have known about some vice he had — gambling or whoring, or what he had done to one of these poor women. He obviously had some hold over him."

"Let me ask something," Juliana said, sitting forward. "Maria, if your parents had known what the earl was capable of, would they still have married you to him?"

"No," she said, shaking her head, hoping she was correct. "I do not believe they would go that far."

Lady Winchester then spoke up, surprising them all. "Warwick — the previous one — would have known of Lord Dennison. He frequented places that would... allow those types of things."

"How do you know?" Juliana asked, her mouth slightly agape.

Her grandmother eyed her with a look. "Have you not learned by now, child, that nothing happens around here without my knowing about it?"

"Perhaps that's it, then," Juliana said. "Maybe Father knew of his proclivities and threatened to spread the rumors. Would it have been enough to provoke Lord Dennison if it meant he would perhaps be unable to find a bride?"

"You don't believe someone would still have been desperate enough to have married off their daughter to him?" Lady Prudence asked. "You know how some of these people are. As long as no one speaks of the goings-on behind closed doors, it never happens."

"That's exactly it, though," Juliana said. "If people spoke of it, it would matter that others would *know* they were greedy enough to marry their daughter to him."

They were all silent as they considered that.

"Well, this mystery certainly has not lacked potential suspects," Matthew said with a wry chuckle. "But I do thank you, Lady Maria, for providing us all of the information you had noted."

"Of course," she said, "I will do anything to help."

Hudson fixed her with a look.

"Anything that will not put any of us — including me — in danger," she amended.

"Thank you," Matthew said, before turning to address the room once more. "I suppose that is all of it, then. If anyone thinks of anything else, please let me know."

They sat for a moment, uncertain of what to do, if they should leave or remain as if they were here on a social visit — this was not exactly a typical situation to find oneself in — when the duke leaned over to Hudson.

"A word?"

Hudson bristled for a moment, but he couldn't very well deny the man.

"Very well."

He followed the duke and Archibald back to Archibald's study as the ladies huddled together in the way that ladies often did.

He didn't take a seat but leaned back in one corner of the neat yet sparsely decorated room.

The duke leaned back against the desk, although he didn't fully sit either.

"This will sound like an odd thing to say, considering our... history," he began, "but I'm worried about you."

Hudson could only stare at him. "For me?"

The duke nodded, as Matthew rounded the desk and took a seat in his chair, observing the two of them.

"It is fortunate that Lady Maria escaped when she did. The earl is as bad as they come. I had an inkling before, and now that I've had the opportunity to ask questions, I have no problem believing the stories the maids have told about him. Juliana had guessed there was something amiss as well, with that instinct of hers. She tried to warn Lady Maria, but she wouldn't go against her family — as most women wouldn't. I suppose I am too used to my sisters and Emma, who seem to be the three women in London with minds of their own."

He rolled his eyes, and Hudson couldn't help a slight chuckle as he knew how much the women vexed the duke, despite how much he loved them in turn.

"I know my grandmother told Lady Maria that she should leave London, and as much as I hate to say it, she is likely right. There is no life for her here. She will always be at risk of being discovered, and I shudder to think what the earl would do if he were to find her."

He looked Hudson right in the eye, disconcerting him as his gaze was so like that which stared back at him from the mirror.

"I know," Hudson said, even as slight panic began to rise within him at the thought of her leaving. "I am doing everything I can to keep her safe."

"But is that enough?" the duke insisted. "If the Earl were to find you, I would do what I could to help you, but he is her husband. We would have no action — within the law, that is — to keep her from him. And Lewis…" his expression turned to one of sympathy, "I have no idea how it occurred, but it is obvious that the two of you care for one another. I do not know if anything has happened between you, and trust me, I am not one to pass judgement if it has, but you have to understand there is no way out of this. Whether or not anyone likes it, she is married, in the eyes of the church and the law, as well as all of society."

"Of course, I understand that," Hudson said. It was what he had kept reminding himself since she had returned to his life. He didn't need the duke coming in and suddenly acting like he was his older brother with all of his worldly advice. He was not even truly the elder, as Hudson bested him there by a few months.

"I do not want to see you hurt, is all," the duke repeated. "If you did truly want to be with her, you would have to leave here, start a new life, one in which no one knew who you were. You'd have to create new identities, pretend you were husband and wife, although you could never be in truth. And it would be uncertain as to whether or not you could continue to practice as a physician."

Hudson nodded curtly. He had certainly thought of this himself. In fact, the idea of making Maria his — at least, as much as she ever could be — was more tempting than the duke could ever realize. There were so many concerns, however. There was the fact he would have to leave his practice and his patients, of course. If he were to start over, he would likely have to say goodbye to his profession. And then there was his mother. Could he really leave her behind, when he was all that she had in the world? He highly doubted that she would come along with him, not when she had worked so hard for the life she had now. And he could never allow her to know he would be leaving behind his profession, not when she had worked half her life to bring it to fruition.

There had to be another way. He just had no idea what that was, and in the meantime, he had to make sure that he didn't lose Maria.

"Thank you for your concern, Your Grace," he said now with a nod of his head to his half-brother, "but I will be sure to handle it — and will keep Maria safe at the same time."

He pushed himself off the wall to leave the office, and the duke called out after him.

"Hudson."

"Yes?" he said without turning around.

"I know I am not your brother in the traditional sense, but I do think you should call me Giles. Or Remington, as many do. Your Grace is not necessary."

"It is when I am a mere commoner, Your Grace, and a bastard at that. Good day to both of you."

He knew he was being rude, but at that point, all he desired was to leave with Maria. He was tired of being reminded of who he was compared to his half-siblings. It would likely have been best had they never found him at all.

CHAPTER 10

*T*he walk home had been a silent one.

Maria could tell that something had bothered Hudson, although she was rather preoccupied with her own concerns.

When they entered Hudson's home, he stepped through the doorway and stopped as though he knew he had to say something to address the discussion.

"Did you have a nice time?"

"A nice time?" she repeated, crinkling her nose. "I do not suppose I would call it a social visit."

"It looked that way when I came out of the office."

She didn't like the surliness in his tone, and she crossed her arms over her chest. "Actually, Lady Prudence and Lady Winchester were telling me how concerned my family was about me."

He snorted. "Then perhaps they shouldn't have married you to a monster."

"I do not believe they realized his true nature."

"They do now," he countered with a shrug. "They should be happy that you escaped."

He had a point, but she didn't like the way he so flippantly made the comment. Her parents were not bad people. They had done as was expected of them — as most would.

"Even so, I cannot help but wish they knew that I was safe," she said. "It all happened so quickly. Just two months ago, I was a single woman, passed over by the duke, yes, but still living in the same house as I always had, with my parents. Now, I am not only married but escaped from my husband — potentially a murderer. I have no idea what I will do with my life except stay hidden from him, and from the sounds of it I might not even be able to remain in England. How could I possibly live alone in a completely foreign country?"

Maria finally closed her lips, embarrassed that it had all come spilling out like that, but it seemed once she began to let her feelings emerge, she couldn't contain them any longer.

She finally stole a glance at Hudson, and his face had softened somewhat.

"I'm sorry, Maria," he said, wiping his hand over his forehead. "I never meant to be callous. I am having difficulty feeling sympathy for the people who put you in such a position. And I—"

"Yes?" she urged him to continue when he winced slightly.

"I had my own conversation with the duke this evening that did not go particularly well. Sometimes being with him is a reminder of how different our lives are, despite sharing a father. He holds such power. Perhaps if I did as well, I could do more for you."

"Hudson," she said, walking over to him, "I hardly think that you could do anything differently than the duke. Neither of you can change what has happened, or break marriage vows already spoken."

"Perhaps not," he said, taking a step in toward her, his eyes no longer on hers, but resting on her lips, which she couldn't help licking at the attention. "But if I had been in his shoes, I most certainly would have married you when I had the chance."

The tension between them finally broke when they stepped into each other, closing the distance between them as they met in a forbidden yet irresistible embrace once again. It was as wonderful as it had been the first time, perhaps even more so, now that they knew more of one another.

His lips were slightly more insistent this time, though still contained a tenderness that she had come to expect from him. They pressed against hers, and soon enough his tongue rested against her lips, which she parted for him, although she jumped slightly when his tongue came between them to search within.

Hudson reacted to her slightest movement, lifting his head, though his breathing was still heavy. "I'm sorry," he said. "Did I scare you?"

"You startled me is all," she said, lifting her hands to his cheeks, his slight scruff scratching her fingertips. "You don't have to stop."

"Are you sure?"

"Absolutely."

He returned his lips to hers then, and this time she would be the one who copied his movements of twirling her tongue against his. He obviously enjoyed it, for his arms tightened around her back, pulling her in closer so that her body was flush against his. He held her against him as he tasted her, drinking her in, until Maria was on fire and all she could think was that she wanted more, that she needed to somehow become closer to him, that only he had what she needed to complete the satisfaction she yearned for.

Even when he leaned back from her, lifting his lips from hers, she clutched at the lapels of his jacket, not wanting to let him go.

"Hudson," she said, her voice hoarse. "I feel... I feel..."

"Desire?"

"*Yes*," she said, deciding that was the exact word to describe how she felt. "It makes me need something — need you — more than I thought possible. I don't know how to ask, or even *what* to ask, I just need... you."

Her cheeks were aflame now as she tried to put into words what she wanted from him, but the problem was, she was not entirely certain *what* she was seeking. She just knew it was not what proper ladies spoke of out loud. Not what proper ladies were supposed to want.

But she was no longer a proper lady. She had lost her reputation, so what did it matter if she no longer acted how she was expected? In losing the life she had known, she finally realized she was gaining something else — the freedom to be the person she wanted to be, not the person she had always been asked to be.

"Oh, Maria," he murmured. "I shouldn't, and yet..." suddenly he smiled wickedly, which sent another streak of heat down between her legs, where she was throbbing for him. "I think there is a way I can fulfill your needs until you've had time to consider what you truly want."

Maria had no idea what he was talking about, but she was willing to let him show her whatever he was suggesting.

He took her hand and wordlessly led her back into the bedroom. She followed along, for once not needing to pretend she was someone else but knowing she was herself, Maria — not Lady Maria, not Lady Dennison, but simply Maria, who was following her own whims.

Even if they went against everything she had ever believed about herself.

Hudson sat down on the bed, opened his legs wide, and then reached out and took Maria's hands, pulling her in closer to him. She wondered for a moment if he had begun this way in order to appear less threatening, but all thoughts were soon chased from her mind as he reached up and took her face in his hands before pulling her lips back down to his. As he kissed her senseless, his hands slid down her body, over her waist, her hips, before they wrapped around her thighs. His arms came around her and he lifted her up before turning and laying her back on the bed. He left her lips then, and she cried out in protest, but he appeared to have other ideas in mind.

Her legs hung off the edge of the bed, and he knelt down beside her, his hands coming to her ankles beneath her skirt before slowly beginning to trace small circles upward, over her skin. They stopped at her knees, and he began to rub his thumbs around them in slow circles as Maria lay back and allowed him to do as he pleased. There was one thing she knew — Hudson's touch brought only pleasure, never pain.

Hudson began to lift her skirts, and when Maria swiftly inhaled, he stopped.

"If there is anything you do not want me to do, Maria, say the word."

"I will," she said, surprised at the huskiness of her tone. "Right now, I do *not* want you to stop."

He gave a low chuckle, the sound going straight through to her core.

"I'm going to put my mouth on you," he said, his voice hoarse. "I'm going to taste you, and you're going to enjoy every minute of it."

"What?" she couldn't help but gasp, suddenly wondering who this man was and what had happened to the calm, demure physician she was used to. His words were so wicked, yet they caused another rush of heat to her center. "I'm not sure—"

"Trust me," he said, and she did, wholeheartedly. "But if it doesn't feel right, say no."

"Very well," she said, finding the air had suddenly vacated her lungs.

The stubble of his chin brushed against the inside of her thigh, and she shivered as it tickled her. His hands rose until they wrapped around her hips, seemingly possessing her. He tucked her skirts, including her chemise, up around her hips and Maria was suddenly completely embarrassed to know that she was bared to him. Goodness, what must he think? He must be—

"You are incredible."

"I'm not," she protested.

"You are," he said. "Everything about you has me intoxicated. It's been a struggle to stay so far from you."

"I didn't know..." Maria could hardly form words, especially when she could feel Hudson's breath on her thigh once more, and she was mortified that he was so close to her.

"You are a mystery in yourself, Maria," he continued, his voice a low, soothing murmur. "You are everything a man could ever want, yet you hide your true self from all but those who know you best."

"That's how it is supposed to be."

"Not here," he said, and she wished she could see his face. "Not with me."

Then he was gone from between her legs and stretched over her once more. He leaned in and kissed her again, drinking her in, overcoming Maria with the sensation that he couldn't get enough of her, which was crazy because she felt the exact same about him. She could feel a hard length against her thigh that she knew must be Hudson, but instead of being terrified, as she had been when her mother had described her wedding night expectations, she instead wanted to know more, wanted to feel more, wanted to discover just what he looked like and how they could fit together.

But for now, she would have to be content with his tongue sliding in and out of her mouth, and she felt like a wanton when she moved her hips against him. She wasn't entirely sure how it began, but soon enough they were moving against each other. The urge Maria had felt earlier to be closer to him pulsed through her once more, and she began to push off the sleeves of his jacket. He let her, pausing for a moment to strip out of it, before his waistcoat and shirt followed, and his torso was bared to her. He was surprisingly well-defined, his muscles sculpted and sinewy, with a light dusting of hair covering him. Maria couldn't help but run her hands over his shoulders, his chest, and then around his back. He groaned as he kissed her again, and then her hands ran lower still until they reached the waistband of his pants.

"Maria," he said, her name on a groan, and she wondered if she had gone further than he would like. Instead of responding, however, he disappeared to kneel in front of her once more.

And then her entire world came apart — but this time in a way that she would welcome, time and again.

His mouth came upon her, warm and wet where she had been pulsing with need for him. She gasped as his tongue moved up and over her, swirling around a sensitive bud that seemed to be prepared for him. Maria couldn't help the moan that escaped her mouth as his tongue ran up one side of her, down the other, then began to circle the small bundle of nerves he easily found once more.

"Oh, Hudson," she cried, and he answered her by licking her again. Maria knew she should be utterly mortified but it was too hard to be so when his mouth was wet and moving against her.

Then he pushed his tongue inside of her and she — the subdued Lady Maria — let out a cry that she couldn't control as she rolled her hips into him. He sped up, slowed down, was hard against her and then soft. As his actions built, so did the intensity of her body. Her fingers clutched the blankets below her, as she rocked her hips faster and faster until—

All of her muscles clenched as tingles spread through her body, air leaving her lungs on a loud shot as she reached down with one hand and held Hudson's head against her.

When she let go, he sat back as well, and they stayed still, staring at one another.

"Hudson," she began, her voice near a croak as she wasn't sure she would be able to speak properly again. She knew she should do something for him in turn but had no idea how to begin. "That was the most amazing thing I've ever felt in my life."

"Good."

"I—I should—"

"You should do nothing. That was for you."

"But—"

"Sometimes, Maria, you need to accept that someone has done something for your pleasure and your pleasure alone. The fact that you enjoyed it is all I need to know."

"I most certainly did. Enjoy it that is."

It seemed such an understatement, but she was so flummoxed she didn't seem to be able to form additional words.

"I'll be right back," he said, and then disappeared out of the room and into his study, leaving Maria staring after him. Where had he gone? Had he been completely disgusted by her? He had said it was for her, but was he regretting his actions? Why was he leaving her alone?

Maria blew out a long, slow breath as she resettled her skirts around her. She was overthinking this, as she always did.

But as she stared at the closed door of his study, she couldn't help but wonder if this was going to change everything.

CHAPTER 11

*H*udson knew he shouldn't have left her like that. If he had remained in the room, however, staring at her with her flushed cheeks, her dishevelled hair, and her clothing in such disarray — all his own doing — he would have spent himself right there in his breeches beside her.

He had no wish to scare her let alone cause her to question if she should have returned his offer, so he had decided the best thing to do was to remove himself alone to his study in order to see to his own desires.

It hadn't taken long.

Yet he couldn't seem to bring himself to return to her once more. What was he to say to her? He had no answer for the future, and he could hardly continue to treat her like… well, a mistress of all things. He knew they had to talk about this, but he was acting the coward.

When he finally emerged, he continued to the bedroom, only to find that she had completely disappeared from it.

"Hudson?"

He turned around rapidly to find her standing there

behind him. She waved a hand to the sofa. "Perhaps we should sit?"

She apparently held much more courage than he did. He nodded stiffly, but instead of taking the seat she had indicated next to her on the sofa, he sat across from her in a chair. What did it say about him that he could not even sit in her proximity without being tempted to take her in a way that would not at all preserve her innocence?

Although who she should preserve it for now, he had no idea.

Maria held her head high as she set her shoulders back and down.

He opened his mouth to apologize, but she held up one hand before he could.

"I sincerely hope the next words out of your mouth are not going to be 'I'm sorry.'"

Hudson shut his lips once more.

"I am not at all sorry for what happened. It was by far the greatest sensation I have ever felt, and the best gift I could ever have asked for."

A sense of pride filled him, although he didn't exactly know how to respond to her.

"I still feel I was in the wrong," he finally couldn't help but say, lifting a hand in supplication. "I took advantage of the vulnerability you were feeling—"

"Were you not of a similar mind as well?"

"Yes, but—"

"Then but nothing," she said. "You also said that if you were the duke, you would have married me. Is that true?"

She asked her question with such straightforwardness, he found that he couldn't lie, no matter what it might mean for the two of them.

"Yes, of course."

She lost some of her stoicism then as her shoulders

dropped and she simply stared at him. "We certainly make a pair, don't we?"

"In what way?"

"We could have made quite the life for ourselves, but we both acted too late."

"Maria," he said, moving off the chair and over to the sofa now, his heart breaking at the crestfallen look in her eyes, "I could never have offered for you. I am a bastard physician. You are the daughter of a marquess."

"And look where I am now," she said, shaking her head. "I enjoyed tonight with every fibre of my being, but I feel... I feel that this is not fair to you. I am staying here as a guest in your home, and for what reason? I have nothing to offer you. And as for what we feel for one another, I cannot be the woman for you. Whether we like it or not, I am married to another."

"I understand," he said immediately, although her words reminded him of what he needed to clarify. "Do not think that what we shared... physically... was expected in any form for repayment of allowing you to be here."

She arched an eyebrow. "Was I not the one on the receiving end of that exchange?"

He couldn't help a soft chuckle. "I have to admit that I rather enjoyed it myself as well."

"You did?" she asked, her eyes widening in apparent fascination.

"I most certainly did," he said, even though he knew that admitting it was a mistake. He sobered somewhat, knowing what it was that he had to say to her now. "I know that the future is unpredictable. But one thing I need you to understand is that I would never hurt you. In fact, I promise to always be there for you, in any manner you require."

"I know," she said, her eyes tearing up once more, and she

rapidly blinked away the moisture. "Perhaps it is best that we enjoy what we have together now."

"Perhaps," he said, even though he knew it was not the best. For he already knew that he would be devastated if she left him, in any way — and she most decidedly would at some point, for she was a woman who deserved the world, even if she had to escape into it. But how could he deny her, or say goodbye to this woman who had captivated him like no other ever had before?

"My innocence—" her face was turning pink again, which was not good news if he was supposed to be keeping himself away from her, "—means nothing anymore. All I am happy about is the fact that my husband did not take it, for I'm sure he would have made it decidedly painful. I would much prefer to give that gift to someone who would appreciate it, perhaps even treasure it."

She looked to him meaningfully now, and Hudson swallowed hard. Surely, she didn't mean—

"Maria, I—"

Before he could continue his sentence, however, there was a knock on the door, and Hudson let out a long sigh. Perhaps if he waited long enough, the person on the other side would leave to find another physician.

But no, the knock came again, and Hudson could at least be grateful that his guest hadn't arrived a short time earlier.

Hudson rose to his feet and opened the door a crack.

"Mrs. Bloomsbury?"

"Dr. Lewis!" she said as though surprised to see him there — in his home.

"Are you unwell?" he asked.

She narrowed her eyes, and he was aware that his greeting lacked a certain amount of enthusiasm, but how could he be pleased to see the woman when he had just pleasured first Maria and then himself and they had been in the midst of discussing what was to come next between them?

When Maria had discussed losing her innocence, had she meant tonight? Another time? He was desperate to know and yet at the same time he needed to do all he could to fill his head with less desirous thoughts — thoughts that would allow him to address whatever concerns the woman had this time. He hoped Maria had made herself scarce behind him. He could only imagine what Mrs. Bloomsbury would have to say to the neighbourhood about his new assistant living with him.

"I am well," Mrs. Bloomsbury said, although she seemed uneasy, shifting her weight from one foot to other, her clothing rather askew. "It is actually my husband. He has taken a turn for the worse."

Mr. Bloomsbury had lost part of his leg in the war. It was a common injury, one that Hudson had treated multiple times, but Mr. Bloomsbury didn't seem to have the spirit to live a more fulfilled life. It was an occurrence that Hudson had seen time and again. It was only in his power to treat the condition, do all he could medically to assist the patient, but if the man or woman didn't have the notion themselves to improve, then there was nothing he could do to bring them fully back to health.

"What seems to be the problem this evening?" he asked.

"He doesn't want to eat anything. I can hardly move him. I tried myself and he... nearly knocked me over."

She actually looked somewhat frightened, and Hudson couldn't help but feel sympathy for her.

"Very well. I will be there shortly."

The Bloomsburys lived just a few houses away, so Hudson had no qualms about allowing Mrs. Bloomsbury to return home unescorted. He would normally have accompanied her, but he didn't want to leave Maria without another word. Mrs. Bloomsbury appeared slightly offended but nodded and thanked him before heading out the door.

He shut it behind her and turned to speak to Maria, but she was no longer on the sofa — she had already risen and was in his study, preparing his bag for him.

"I can do that," he said, but she shook her head.

"I don't mind," she said, holding it out to him with a shy smile. "I hope I gathered everything you need."

He nodded, slightly astonished. He hadn't realized how closely she paid attention to his work.

"You don't have to attend tonight. Mr. Bloomsbury can become... unpredictably angry."

"A result of his war experience, I expect," she said with more understanding than he would have thought possible with her sheltered upbringing.

"How did you—"

"People try to hide their realities, but I've seen many a man affected by war," she said. "Mrs. Bloomsbury might need help or at least company. I don't mind. Truly."

"Very well," he said. "I'll leave first and make sure she isn't waiting out front."

Maria nodded as Hudson checked the door before waving her forward and they quickly reached the Bloomsburys' home.

"You summoned your assistant without much notice," Mrs. Bloomsbury said, looking from Hudson to Maria with some suspicion, but before she could voice any suppositions or conclusions, there was a bellow of rage behind them, and she cringed. "He seems to be in a great deal of pain," she said, and Hudson hurried on back into the bedroom.

"Mr. Bloomsbury," he said to the man thrashing about. "Your wife tells me that you are not feeling like yourself."

The man began muttering about the French approaching, as Hudson did all he could to placate him while opening his bag and taking out a bottle of laudanum. He would try to ease the man's nerves at least, to take some of the edge off. He would assess the man's leg and ensure there was no festering, but the unfortunate reality was that Mr. Bloomsbury's true ailment was nothing he could fix with any medications or surgeries.

He sat with Mr. Bloomsbury as he calmed, then continued his examination and was just finishing when Maria called out to him.

"Dr. Lewis?"

"Yes?" he said, coming to the door, where Maria met him. She leaned in, her voice hushed.

"I believe Mrs. Bloomsbury is injured. Perhaps it was when she tried to help her husband, or perhaps he accidentally injured her, but I suspect you should check that nothing is amiss with her."

"I'll be right there," he said, and she nodded.

A short time later he explained to Mrs. Bloomsbury that her husband was resting, and then suggested she see the apothecary and ask for laudanum to help when the fits began.

"How are you doing, Mrs. Bloomsbury?" he asked nonchalantly. "Is the shoulder still bothering you?"

She hesitated. "Yes, slightly," she said, and it was then he noticed the bruises on her arm.

"Let's take a look over here," he said gently, leading her over to the sofa, and when he opened his bag he noticed that he had forgotten one of his tools in the bedroom.

"One moment. It appears one of my syringes fell out of my bag."

"I'll find it," Maria said, already walking back. The door was open, and Mr. Bloomsbury was sleeping, so Hudson let her go without comment.

He was just assessing the movement of Mrs. Bloomsbury's shoulder when there was a shout from the bedroom, and he was moving before he even realized he was doing so.

"Maria?" he called out, and when he entered the room, he froze in the doorway when he saw Mr. Bloomsbury out of bed, holding Maria's back against him, his arm wrapped around her neck.

Mr. Bloomsbury may have been practically bedridden for quite some time, but he had a strength about him that frightened Hudson — especially with Maria in his grip.

Hudson's vision seemed to narrow in on them as he tried to determine the best way to extricate her without causing her any harm. He heard Mrs. Bloomsbury enter behind him as she let out a shriek herself, but he didn't have time to see to her — he was too focused on Maria and his own panic at what Mr. Bloomsbury might do.

"Harold, stop this at once!" Mrs. Bloomsbury called out with both anger and desperation, but her husband was too far gone. He let out a snarl in response as his head snapped one way and then the next. Maria's eyes were wide in fear, but she didn't thrash about. She simply stood there, still, waiting for either Hudson to help her or for Mr. Bloomsbury to release her.

"Mr. Bloomsbury," Hudson said in as calm a voice he could manage considering what was happening in front of him, "you are home. You are safe. Maria here poses no threat."

"Traitor," he snarled. "Here to gut us all!"

"She is a friend, Mr. Bloomsbury. We all are. We just want to help you."

"Stay away!" he shouted back, but his grip seemed to be loosening, even while his eyes roved from one side to the other as though he was trying to determine what was reality and what was part of his own imaginings.

"I'm going to come closer to you, Mr. Bloomsbury, and I

will take Maria, all right? I will ensure that you are safe, that no one will harm you."

He inched ever closer, and then with a big huff, Mr. Bloomsbury practically hurled Maria out of his arms and toward Hudson. Hudson caught her to him, holding her close, and as he breathed in her scent and felt her melt into his body, he made a vow, even though he knew it would be impossible to uphold. He would never let her go again.

CHAPTER 12

*M*aria tried to keep up with Hudson, but he had such a tight grip around her shoulders it was nearly impossible to do so.

"Hudson," she said, her breath coming in short pants, but his head was down, his eyes on the ground ahead of him, as he moved with such purpose that she assumed he hadn't heard her.

"Hudson!" she repeated, more loudly now, and he stopped so abruptly that she nearly fell forward from the momentum.

She took a breath as she moved in front of him, her hands coming to his shoulders.

"Can you please slow down?" she asked as his breath was still coming rather quickly. "I am fine."

"I know you are fine," he said, wiping a hand over his face as he hefted his bag higher on his shoulders. "But you could have—he could have—"

"But he didn't," she said firmly, linking her arm through his this time instead of having him drag her forward. "Come. Let's go home."

He nodded and before long they were entering the house.

As soon as the door shut behind them, he dropped his bag to the ground and turned around toward her, gathering her up his arms and holding her close.

While Maria was aware the embrace was for his own comfort as much as it was for hers, she enjoyed being wrapped so securely in his arms.

He finally let go, his eyes searching hers as though reassuring himself once more that she truly was unharmed.

"I'm sorry, Maria, I was just... terrified that he had done something to hurt you, that I could have lost you again."

"I seem to be putting you through quite a few trials, am I not?"

He chuckled lowly as he rubbed his eyes before turning from her for a moment.

"Maria," he said, her name emerging as a groan. "I just... I cannot imagine my life without you. In any way. How bad is that?"

She stepped closer to him, her heart near to bursting out of her chest at how much this man wanted her, cared for her, in a way that she never thought would be possible for her — especially not now.

"It is not bad at all," she said, reaching up and lifting a stray lock of hair from his forehead, pushing it back but keeping her hand cupped around his temple. "It is the truth. *Our* truth. And I thank you."

"For what?" he said, dropping his hands, staring at her in astonishment.

"For all that you do for me. For how much you care."

"Oh, Maria," he said, taking her face in his hands. "I cannot help but care. Far more than I should."

He leaned down, then, pressing his lips against hers, gently at first, but then more forcibly, with a hunger that she would hardly be able to fathom — except that she felt the exact same way.

He began to back up and she followed, their lips still locked, until he was the one sitting back on the bed this time. The sun had set, and the room was lit by only the soft glow of embers from the hearth where the fire had been burning before Mrs. Bloomsbury had called on them.

So much had been left unsaid between them, and now it all came bursting forward. Hudson lifted Maria so that her legs were wrapped around him. Her skirts were bunched between them, and he lifted them to her waist with one hand while stroking the silky skin of her leg with the other, gripping her firm bottom when he reached it.

"Do you want this?" he asked, his voice desperate with need, yet still, he gave her the choice, the control.

"Yes," she answered resolutely. She did. With him, and only him. It might not be fair, it might not be right, but it was what they both needed from one another. She had always lived for the future but since escaping her marriage, she was living for the moment. And there had never been more of a moment than this right now.

Her arms wrapped around his neck as she gave herself over to him, losing herself in his taste, his touch. He had both hands around her bottom now, and when he squeezed, she couldn't keep herself from lowering more fully into him. Even as his hard length pressed against her, she felt no fear — only the need for more.

She leaned back for a moment to push his jacket off of his shoulders, wanting to see more of him again. Hudson helped her, slipping it off, before adding his waistcoat to the pile on the floor. She undid the top few buttons of his linen shirt before he discarded that as well.

Once he was undressed, he went to work on the buttons at the back of her dress, and after a few clumsy motions, together they wrestled it off of her body and onto the floor. Her undergarments and chemise soon followed, until her body was bare to his. She felt rather exposed, especially with his eyes fixated in front of him on her chest, but from what she could tell, he seemed to like what he saw.

"Maria," he breathed. "You are absolutely beautiful."

She pushed away the strands of hair that had fallen over her shoulders when they had removed her clothing, interested in just what he had lying in wait for her but uncertain exactly how to explore it.

She put one hand on his chest before beginning to trail her fingers lower, until they sat on the top of the waistband of his breeches, and while she had been wanting this — him — she was suddenly frozen by uncertainty of what to do next.

Hudson sensed her hesitancy and took her hand in his, bringing it to his length on top of his breeches, moving her hand in his over him, rubbing up and down. His eyes closed as his head dropped backward, and soon enough Maria found the rhythm herself, enjoying the fact that her touch could elicit such a response from him. She experimentally squeezed, and he groaned, reaching up and running his hands over her waist to come beneath her breasts.

He cupped them with his fingers as he reached up and stroked her nipples with his thumbs. She let out a gasp as she arched into him, and just when she was becoming used to his touch, his mouth closed over one of her breasts and he began to stroke her nipple with his tongue.

"Hudson!" she exclaimed as she leaned further into him, her hips moving over top of him in time. She had no idea if what she was doing was right, but it felt marvelous, and he didn't make any motion to stop her.

He lifted her up and stood so that he could slide his breeches down his legs, and it was then Maria stopped and could only stare.

ELLIE ST. CLAIR

"Maria?" he said, stepping closer and bringing his index finger underneath her chin. "Are you all right?"

"Yes, I… I'm just not sure…"

"What is it, love?"

"You are—it is—very large."

"Well, thank you," he said with a chuckle.

"I'm just not sure how something like that can fit in…"

"I know," he said, leaning down and kissing her lips quickly, softly. "We'll go slow. I promise. Say the word if you want me to stop."

She managed a nod before she reached down and tentatively stroked his bare skin this time. His swift intake of breath told her that he liked it, and she continued to slide her hand back and forth over his soft, velvety skin as he sat back on the bed, allowing her to explore her fill before he pushed her too quickly.

"Hudson?"

"Yes?"

"What you did to me earlier… can I do the same to you?"

"The same? You mean you want to use your mouth?"

She nodded as heat rushed to her cheeks.

"If that is what you want, far be it from me to deny you," he said. "But do not feel that you have to."

"I want to," she said, and realized that she truly meant it. She did. She wanted to give him the same pleasure he had brought her, and if it would feel just as good for him, then she was happy to do it.

She could feel his gaze upon her as she leaned down and placed her tongue on the tip of him. She had no idea what she was supposed to do, but she thought of how his tongue had moved on her, and she swirled hers around him likewise. Hudson groaned, his breathing becoming heavier, and she wrapped her lips around him before taking a look up at him for assurance she was doing it right.

"My word, Maria," he said, and he gently moved her head ever so slightly until she understood the rhythm. He surprised her by thrusting slightly into her mouth, his fingers wrapping in her hair.

Finally with a groan, he pulled her off him, bringing her up his body, and took her mouth with his lips again. Maria opened to him, and as he slid his tongue in, his hand began to stroke her between her legs. He caressed that place that caused such pleasure, and then he slowly began to slide a finger inside her. Maria froze for a moment, causing him to do so as well, until she began to rock into him, asking for more.

He pushed his fingers deeper, and when she began to move her hips against him, he continued to rub her as well. Maria sighed into his mouth, and then he was turning her over, laying her gently on the bed in front of him. He climbed up, his arms around her head as he leaned over her, and she knew that it was almost time. She fought the panic, which was slightly growing although not nearly as strongly as her desire for him.

"Are you all right? You do want this?" he asked again, and she nodded. She did.

He slid slightly inside her entrance and there was a flash of pain, though he was slow, gentle, and had only placed a small bit of himself within. He leaned down and kissed her again, which helped her to relax and take her mind off any discomfort.

He slid further into her, bit by bit, until his body was against her and he was seated fully within her.

Hudson leaned back and rained tender kisses all over her face. Maria looked up into his eyes.

"How does that feel?" he asked, and she shifted experimentally.

"I think it feels all right now."

"Are you sure?"

"Yes," she said, which was enough reassurance for him to begin to rock against her. He went in and out before stopping, raising an eyebrow as he looked down at her.

She nodded, and he thrust again, a little harder, a little deeper before studying her another time.

"Oh, yes, that feels good," she cried this time as she gripped his shoulders, and he began a slow, gentle thrusting. Maria's body responded of its own accord, her hips moving with his, and she let out a small moan that seemed to encourage him to increase his speed — which she was certainly glad of, for the more he moved, the better it was feeling.

"Oh, Hudson," she groaned, and he sat back and lifted her legs slightly, his eyes down on where they were joined. Then his hand came to her again and he began to rub slow circles. She found the excitement within her body beginning to build once more, until she was crying out with the exquisiteness of all that was coursing through her.

Then he leaned forward and took her mouth again as he thrust harder into her, and she gripped her fingers into his back as suddenly the sensations overtook her and she was crying out. She hardly registered him burying his face into her neck as he thrust harder than he had from the start, gripping her against him as he seemed to lose himself in her.

When he had finished, they stayed locked together, catching their breath, yes, but Maria also needed the time to understand all that had just happened between them. She had thought she was close to Hudson before, that she felt such a connection with him but now... now that she knew what it truly meant to be with him, she never wanted to look back.

It also scared her, knowing how tied to him she was. Here she had left her life to look after herself, and she had fallen into Hudson's arms. Now that she was there, she never wanted to leave.

Hudson finally lifted himself up onto his elbows as he pushed a strand of hair away from her face while staring at her with a tenderness that she wasn't sure she deserved but welcomed all the same.

"That was... incredible," she breathed.

"It was more than I ever thought possible," he said, although there was a hint of worry in his eyes.

"What's wrong?" she asked.

"It's only... I should know better than anyone what a joining like this can mean. I became lost in you, in the moment, but I should have had the sense to have taken more precaution."

"I see," she said. She should have thought of that herself. "Well, I suppose all we can do now is what we have been doing since I arrived."

"Which is?"

"Take things as they come, one day at a time, one moment at a time. If there is a... consequence, then we will determine what we should do then."

"You're right," he said, although he didn't appear convinced. "I just... I don't want to be the same man my father was. I would marry you if I could, but—"

Maria gripped his face between her hands, staring deep into his eyes, needing him to understand.

"I know. You are nothing like your father, do you understand me? No matter what happens, I know you would never do anything to hurt me. I trust you."

"I will always look after you," he said fiercely.

She nodded, tears filling her eyes. She knew he would never break that promise, but the question was — could she truly ask that of him?

CHAPTER 13

*H*udson couldn't keep himself from touching Maria the next day. They had spent the night wrapped in one another's arms, though the truth of the situation had rendered him unable to sleep as he considered all of the options. She might never be able to be his wife in name, but that didn't mean he couldn't make her his in every other way possible. He had no idea what that would look like — where they would go or how he could continue practicing as a physician or what to do about his mother — but they would make it work. They had to.

For he didn't think he could live without her any longer.

Today when he was doing his rounds, he no longer cared if any of his patients guessed that she was more than his assistant. He could have lost her last night — hell, he could have lost her to her husband before he had even found her — but damned if he would ever risk her being taken from him again.

He was fortunate enough to be on the receiving end of her secret smiles that were just for him, and he wondered how he could be so lucky as to be the one favored with her attention. He wasn't sure he would ever become used to it.

But he would damn well try.

Hudson was twining his fingers through hers as they returned home from a call, wondering how much time they might have alone before he would be summoned again, when he stopped, noticing a small package wrapped in brown paper sitting on his doorstep.

"What is that?" he murmured, stepping forward to pick up, and Maria bent her head near his to inspect it herself.

He stared up at her in surprise. "It has your name on it."

"Mine?" she said, wrinkling her nose. "That is… odd. No one knows I am staying here, do they?"

"No," he shook his head. "Not besides the Remingtons. Or my mother, and she has been gone for several days now. Besides, while she might like to ask questions, she certainly wouldn't tell anyone that you are here."

Maria bit her lip, and he could see the worry in her eyes.

"We'll take this in and determine who left it, all right?"

She nodded, and he wrapped an arm around her back as he unlocked the door, taking a quick look around once they entered to make sure there was no one within, but all looked as they had left it.

Perhaps he was overthinking things.

He gave her the package to unwrap, although he stayed nearby in case there was anything harmful within it. Underneath the paper was a small wooden box, and Maria let out a small gasp when she revealed what was within — an intricate necklace, although it didn't appear to be a necklace in a traditional sense.

"This looks costly," she murmured, plucking it from its packaging and draping it over her fingers. Hudson nodded, agreeing. She looked up and met his eyes. "Do you suppose I have an admirer? One of your patients, perhaps?"

His brow furrowed as he examined the gems within their settings. He was no expert on pieces of jewellery, but he had a hard time imagining that any of his patients could afford such a piece.

"Do you mind if I look at it more closely?" he asked, reaching out a hand, and she placed the necklace into it. Most of the stones were diamonds and rubies, interspersed within gold settings. But it was what hung off the necklace he most wanted to see. Just behind the clasp, trailing down the back of the piece, was a chain that didn't seem to fit with the rest of it.

"Maria," he said, uncertain if he should tell her his suspicion but knew she deserved the truth. "I don't think this is a necklace."

"Then what would it be?" she asked, her eyes wide.

"I think it is a collar."

"A collar? Such as one an animal would wear?"

"I believe so."

She took a swift intake of breath as she realized the implications of such a gift.

"How would he know I am here?" she asked, her voice thin.

"I have no idea," he said, shaking his head as he tried to push away the unease that settled over him. "Certainly, none of the duke's family would tell anyone, nor would my mother. Perhaps a patient recognized you from the newspaper? I doubt anyone knows that you are staying here; however, I would be the closest contact anyone would currently have to you."

She nodded, biting her lip, but Hudson could see that it was trembling slightly. He wished he had a way to help her truly feel safe, to protect her from any peril, and he would do his damndest to make sure that nothing and no one would threaten her again. He couldn't help but feel he was already failing in that regard.

For what he wanted most was to remove the threat completely.

"What's this?" she asked, looking beyond the damned collar to the table below, picking up a piece of fine paper that sat upon it.

"An invitation," he said, cursing to himself. He had meant to hide it so that she wouldn't see it.

"The Duchess of Warwick has invited you to a ball," she said, reading it. "It's in two days' time."

"Yes, but it doesn't matter."

"Why not?"

"I will not be attending."

She was looking up at him in some consternation. "Can I ask why?"

He shrugged. "Many reasons. I do not want to leave you alone for one, *especially* now, and I have no interest in attending anyway. I may have initially had a relationship with the Remington family, but it became very clear where I stood with them when the duke accused me of murdering his father and abducting his sister."

Maria nodded slowly as she placed the invitation back down on the table.

"I understand that. Although I do believe that the duke regrets what he said to you. He was desperate to find a solution to what was threatening his family. He absolutely should not have blamed you, but he has apologized, many times over."

"Are you on his side?" Hudson couldn't help but ask, irked that she would defend the man she had been supposed to marry.

"No," she shook her head. "I will always be on *your* side.

Which is why I am urging you to go. I know how much it means to Juliana to have met you and welcomed you into the family. It says a great deal that they would invite you to such an event."

"Yes, most families would never invite their bastard brother," he said with animosity in his voice that he could not help.

"That's actually the truth," she said without comment on his words or his tone. "I am not saying to necessarily forgive and forget everything that has happened, but they do appear to want you in their lives."

He sighed as he ran a hand through his hair. "Even if all of that were true, I cannot leave you alone," he said. "And of course, you could never attend with me."

"No, but perhaps I could stay with someone you trust? Smith, perhaps?"

Hudson frowned. Smith was a good man, and he did consider him and his wife friends, but he had difficulty trusting Maria with anyone other than himself.

She stepped closer to him and placed a hand on his arm. It was difficult to think of anything except making love to her again when she was so near.

"Hudson."

She looked up into his eyes, standing so close that he could smell her lemon-freshness. "When I ran from Lord Dennison, I thought that I would have to find a way to look after myself. I had no plan, only a thought to find Juliana for some clothing and help in determining where I should go. Then, somehow, I found my way to you. And I am ever so glad of it. But I am capable of looking after myself as well. I am sure that for one evening I will be completely fine. And if I am with a friend of yours, how would anyone ever know where to find me, *if* there is even someone who would possibly come looking for me?"

Which, obviously, there was. Hudson didn't like the idea,

but she also had a point. And he knew that if he were to continue to tell her what to do, to place expectations upon her, then she might feel trapped to the point that she would run again — only this time *from* him.

"I will consider attending," he said instead, though he held up a finger. "If I do go, we must ensure that you have somewhere safe to stay, and I would only accept the invitation with the purpose to learn more about your husband and what he has been saying about you. If he does know that I am with you, then I am certain that my appearance at the same event as he would not go without comment."

"Very true," she acknowledged, before stepping closer to him, tilting her head up to him and placing a kiss on his lips. "You are very attractive when you become protective, do you know that?"

He snorted. "Am I now?"

"You are."

He began to back her up to the bedroom. "I'm going to wash off and then I will show you just how *protective* I can be."

She laughed and hurried back to the room. Hudson stared after her, unmoving for a moment as he considered what a lucky man he truly was.

* * *

"Maria! How lovely to see you."

"Thank you," Maria said with a smile as she stepped into the door. Mrs. Smith seemed a kind woman, and she appreciated the couple with their young children opening their home to her for the evening. They hadn't commented on the rather odd request for her to join them, but she supposed that most people in the area felt that they owed Hudson, as the physician, as many favors as they could provide.

"I hope you're hungry," she said, welcoming her into the small house that was of a similar size to Hudson's, but much more of a home.

As Maria sat, two small children appeared at her skirts to make her acquaintance. Their mother tried to wave them away, but Maria told her that it was fine as she knelt to greet them.

In truth, they were a welcome distraction. She hadn't been able to think of much but Hudson since he had left for Warwick House, although he had done so quite reluctantly. She wondered if he would meet anyone there, if he would dance with anyone, and while she had no wish to be in the ballroom herself, she wondered if Hudson would have a desire to join such a life if he had the opportunity.

What would she possibly do if he did?

CHAPTER 14

*W*hat did it mean that the outlandish façade of Warwick House was becoming rather familiar to Hudson? When he stepped through the front doors, he certainly didn't feel like he was coming home by any means, but he also no longer felt like a stranger entering an unwelcome foreign land.

"Dr. Lewis, I am so glad you could come."

The Duchess of Warwick, formerly Lady Emma, greeted him with two hands outstretched. She was a comely woman, with light hair and striking features, kind and rather intriguing from what he knew of her, but he could not begin to understand how a man could choose her — or any other woman, for that matter — over Maria.

Although he was certainly glad the duke had done so.

"How could I ever resist?" he responded as lightly as he could, although he was aware that neither duchess nor duke was fooled by his glib words, and he reminded himself he needed their assistance tonight.

The duke nodded to him next, although he remained somewhat aloof, perhaps unsure of what Hudson's reaction to him would be. Hudson was rather unsure himself, but he fixed a smile on his face, for tonight, he had to set his pride to the side in order to ask for the duke's help — for Maria.

"I thank you, Your Grace, for the invitation," he added to his initial remark toward the duchess before turning to her husband.

"I understand you have many commitments this evening, Your Grace, but if you have a spare moment, could I perhaps have a quick word?"

He raised an eyebrow in question and the duke nodded after a quick flash of surprise crossed his face.

"When we are done greeting our new arrivals, I will come find you," he promised.

Hudson remained in the shadows of the ballroom. Had he not the reason to come here to learn more about the earl and what was being said about Maria's disappearance, he would never have attended. He could not imagine a man more out of place than he was here. If these people were aware of his true identity. As the duke's bastard, they would do far more than glance at him curiously.

He had been to one such event before, yet somehow, he hadn't had the same sense of urgency to depart, and now he could admit the reasoning for it — Maria had been in attendance. He had not been able to speak to her, to dance with her, for he'd had no wish to create any scandal in her life at the time, but he had, at least, been in the same room with her for a few hours, which had been worth any sense of discomfort.

Now, he wished he was by her side again — although he was quite glad she was not here with him given the circumstances. Did she miss her life? Was she waiting for the day when she would hopefully be able to re-enter it once more? He knew she had no wish to leave to the Americas or elsewhere in England, but how much was she regretting coming and staying with him?

True to his word, Hudson hardly had enough time to locate a glass of brandy before the duke appeared at his side.

"I appreciate the excuse," his half-brother murmured as he joined him with a drink of his own. "I hate these things."

"That, I can understand," Hudson responded.

He was already at the outskirts of the room, but he and the duke moved by unspoken agreement further into the shadows.

"I am going to assume that your appearance here this evening is not simply to further your social connections amongst the *ton*," the duke said dryly, to which Hudson snorted.

"Hardly. Although I am here to learn more about certain *members* of the *ton*."

"Dennison," the duke said, his face darkening. "He was not on our invitation list until Prudence suggested that perhaps it is best to keep our enemies closer."

"Your sister is a smart one."

"Too smart," the duke said with a snort. "Would you like an introduction to the earl?"

"No, I do not believe he would ever reveal anything to me as a friendly acquaintance. Especially considering my station," Hudson said. "If you could identify him, however, I may have other ways of learning more."

"Very well," the duke said. "He is there, across the room, leaning over a blond woman."

Hudson followed his finger and quickly spotted the earl, his blood beginning to pound harder through his veins at the sight of him. He certainly did not appear a man concerned for the whereabouts of his missing wife.

The duke fixed a worried look on him.

"What are you going to do?"

"Nothing. At least, not tonight," Hudson said through gritted teeth, his mind already wandering to potions and poisons, though he knew he would never follow through and actually do anything with them. He was a physician, and he had vowed to help people, not to hurt them — no matter how hideous they were.

"Be careful," the duke said worriedly. "If I were to cause injury to another member of the peerage, that is one trial. If *you* were to do so, that would be another circumstance entirely. It would matter to no one what the earl has done."

Hudson looked him square in the face. "Do you believe me stupid?" he retorted.

"Not at all," the duke said, Hudson's response not bothering him in the least.

"Have you heard any talk of Maria tonight?"

"Not a thing," the duke said, only showing brief surprise that Hudson had dropped her title.

"The earl is coming this way," Hudson murmured as he saw the man begin a turn about the room with a young lady. "Is that not scandalous, his flirting with another young lady while his wife has gone missing?"

"It would be, except that he has decided to continue living his life as though he was never married at all," the duke said, disbelief on even his face as he waved his drink toward him. "He has not entered mourning and he does not act as though he was married. But who is going to judge him? Mothers are already considering him as a future husband for their daughters, as he has been making it clear to anyone who asks that he believes his wife is no longer in this world."

"At least she is no longer in *his* world," Hudson said, gripping his drink tighter as his jaw set.

The duke looked over at him. "You truly are a lost man for her, aren't you?"

"Pardon me?"

"You've fallen for her. It's fine. There's no shame in it. As long as you understand the reality of the situation."

"Trust me, I am far more aware than you can imagine," Hudson said through gritted teeth. "And as it happens, I am tired of the big brother act. You are not any older than I am, as it is."

"Born in the same year though, if I recall," the duke said, unfazed.

"Yes. Months apart."

"I, however, know this life, Lewis. I am not saying that makes me any wiser, and, likely, you know far more of the world than I do. But I know *this* world. These people. The power they wield, due to the circumstances of their birth. I do not want you to put your hopes into something that can never be."

"All I need from you is your help in proving Dennison is guilty of murder," Hudson said. "In the meantime, if I can help you learn more about the threat to your family through him, I am happy to do so. It can be of benefit to both of us."

The duke fixed him with a stare.

"Very well, but I'd like you to know that I would do this anyway. I would like you and Lady Maria to find peace."

"It's your fault she is in this situation, anyway," Hudson couldn't help but grumbling, knowing he was being an ass but not particularly caring anymore.

"I do," the duke said, his head dropping in some chagrin. "But would it be any better if she was married to me and we were both simply existing, not living the lives we were meant to live with the people we love?"

Hudson stared out at the swirling colors before him on the dance floor, unable to look the duke in the eye, knowing he was right but unwilling to admit it at first.

"Yes," he said finally. "I suppose you have a point."

They both ceased talking when the earl stopped in front

of them, only he no longer had the young lady on his arm. Instead, he was walking with a man, one Hudson didn't recognize but appeared to be of similar age to him and the duke.

"Who is that?" he asked in a low voice.

"Lord Trundelle," the duke said. "He's a marquess, a bachelor."

"A friend of yours?"

"No," the duke said with a firm shake of his head. "Although, I cannot say I have moved in these circles for long. But from what I know, he isn't the sort I would trust my sister with, although many of the mothers have considered him as a potential husband for years — title and age and all. He, however, has never shown a whit of interest in any of the young ladies, choosing instead I suppose to leave his line to his younger brother, who already has a brood three sons deep. At least, this is what my mother and sisters tell me."

"I see."

They were silent then as the men unknowingly moved close enough for Hudson and the duke to overhear their conversation.

"Is it coming along?" Trundelle asked, and Dennison leaned back against the marble pillar in front of Hudson, the cherubs dancing just above his head as though they were mocking him and his true self.

"Hopefully soon."

"You told me that this would happen quickly, now that old Warwick is gone. It's been more than a year, man."

Hudson sensed the duke stiffen beside him.

"I thought it would be quick as well, but then Remington stepped in sooner than I thought he would, and he got rid of Stone."

"Stone was my father's man-of-business," the duke murmured to Hudson.

Interesting.

"Does he know about the debts?"

"Doubtful. He has never said a word. He would likely have cashed them in by now."

"Can you not hire a man to look into it, to get back the vowels? Soon enough Remington will find them and then we will have no options left," Trundelle's frustration was apparent.

"I do not have the funds to do so," Dennison said through gritted teeth.

"I thought that's why you married the chit," Trundelle said, and Dennison turned to him, anger on his face now.

"I did," he seethed. "And then she took off on me."

"What did you do?"

"Nothing. That is the problem. I should have made sure she subjected to me before she could go anywhere. Then she would have known that she had no option to leave me."

Hudson's hands curled into fists at his side at Dennison's words, but now was not the time to act on anything. The duke shot him a warning look.

"Could we approach Remington, try to give him a story to explain what happened?"

"No," Dennison said quickly. "He would never agree to release the debts."

"He and his father were not on good terms. Everyone knows that."

"No one wants to part with money, Dennison. Not even if it's dirty money from a man he hated."

Hudson wondered whether that was completely true, considering how much he knew Remington had despised the man who had sired them, but he wasn't about to ask him.

"What about the threats to the family? Could we scare the current duke into releasing the debts?"

It was Dennison now who posed the question, and Trundelle turned to him in disbelief.

"Are you an idiot? Then he will assume we are the ones who are threatening him."

"Perhaps we could do it in a way that he wouldn't know our identities. Provide him a list of all of the debts that were owed to the former duke and tell him to release them all or else someone would come for him or one of his sisters again."

"No one will get to the Lady Juliana, not now that the wanton is with the detective."

It was the duke's turn to become offended, although Hudson was not particularly pleased with the sentiment either, for he rather liked his half-sister, who had always been the most welcoming to him of all of the Remington siblings.

"There are ways," Dennison said, and Hudson and the duke exchanged a look at that.

"Dennison, you better come up with it soon. I cannot wait forever."

"You are as deep into this mess as I am."

"And whose fault is that?"

The two men in front of them glowered at one another, and Hudson had the feeling that whatever was tying them together, it certainly wasn't friendship.

They went their separate ways then, leaving Hudson and the duke staring after them.

"What do you make of all of that?" Hudson asked the duke, who shook his head slowly.

"The list of people who could have done away with my father just keeps getting longer, is what I think," he said. "I'll have to talk to Archibald, have him look further into Dennison and Trundelle, see what he can find out."

"Dennison never mentioned Maria, besides for the reason

he married her," Hudson noted, to which the duke shook his head.

"No, but do not let that ease your mind, for chances are high that he has someone trying to find her. Be on your guard, Lewis."

"Of course."

"Now come, I'll introduce you to Lady Bennington."

"Lady Bennington?"

"Lady Maria's mother."

CHAPTER 15

*H*udson was well aware of who Lady Bennington was — in fact, he had even briefly met her in the past.

But not only was he sure she likely had no interest in becoming acquainted with him once more, he could not see what purpose it might serve.

But the duke, apparently, thought otherwise.

The decision was taken out of both of their hands, however, when the duke's name was called out, and the duke turned around to find his mother staring at the two of them in consternation.

She was standing within a trio of women. Hudson recognized one of them as Lady Bennington, the other a woman he had only seen in passing.

"Mother, you look beautiful tonight, as you always do," the duke said, leaning in and kissing his mother on each of her cheeks. The dowager duchess, however, could not seem to remove her eyes from Hudson, and he wondered if she had been aware that he had been included on the guest list.

"Mother, you remember Dr. Lewis?"

"Yes," she said with a curt nod. "Good evening."

Hudson bowed slightly. "Good evening, Your Grace."

"Lady Bennington, Lady Hemingway, may I introduce Dr. Lewis?" the duke said to the two other women standing next to him.

The two women stared wordlessly for a moment, and Hudson hid his smirk as he bowed slightly again. "Good evening. It is a pleasure to make your acquaintance."

They could not politely ignore him and murmured their replies, looking to the duke's mother for guidance on just what they were supposed to do with the bastard physician who had shown up in the middle of her family's *ton* event.

Of course, as far as he knew, they were not actually aware that he was the duke's bastard, but Hudson knew, and that was enough.

"I am sorry to hear about the disappearance of your daughter, Lady Bennington," he said, unsure of whether it was the polite thing to say but hoping to achieve his purpose of determining just how distraught she might be about her daughter's disappearance.

"Thank you," she said curtly, and the slight sheen of water in her eyes told him that she likely did have some true emotion over Maria, although it could also be an act. She *had* married her off to the earl, had she not? "We are hoping that she is returned to us very soon."

Hudson nodded, unsure of how to respond to that, although he noted that the countess made it sound as though someone had taken Maria and that she hadn't run of her own accord — which he supposed made sense, for from what Maria told him, she had never gone against her parents' wishes at any point in time before.

"The poor girl," Lady Hemingway said, sighing dramatically. "I do hope the detectives are able to discover her whereabouts soon. And her poor husband."

Hudson swallowed his opinion on that regard, especially when the duke eyed him with a look.

"I am sure the earl is most distraught," he said instead, attempting to prevent sarcasm from entering his tone. He didn't miss the dowager duchess eyeing him with frank curiosity, and he had a feeling she knew more than she was letting on.

"Oh, yes, he seems the epitome of sorrow," came a new voice, and Hudson turned to see Lady Winchester join the circle. The dowager duchess closed her eyes for a moment as she took a large sip from her drink — likely because her mother appeared to disguise nothing about how she truly felt about the earl.

"Mother," the dowager duchess began, but Lady Winchester waved her words away.

"Do not try to shush me, Elizabeth. Look at the man. Dancing with young women, drinking, flirting. I hardly think he is overwrought about his wife."

Lady Bennington let out a gasp of shock and Lady Winchester eyed her with a knowing look.

"Just because everyone is pretending he is someone else does not change his true character, Lady Bennington. Besides, you married your daughter off to him. What did you expect?"

"Mother, may I please speak to you for a moment?" the dowager duchess said in a strangled voice before pulling her mother away, but not before Lady Winchester surreptitiously winked at Hudson and he nearly choked on his drink as the duke hid a laugh behind his hand.

"Have a wonderful evening," the duke managed, before he backed out of the conversation with Hudson following.

As soon as they were out of earshot of the ladies, the two of them could no longer hold back their chuckles, and Hudson had to admit that, despite all he felt towards the duke, he appreciated being able to share something with him besides animosity and a father.

"I do not suppose you would share a joke with a fellow, would you?"

They looked up to find another man join them, one who Hudson recognized as the duke's relative — son of his father's cousin, Lord Hemingway. The duke made the introductions once more, and Hudson wondered how much his own relation actually knew about his origins, although the man said nothing on the subject.

"Simply my grandmother saying exactly what everyone is thinking, but that no one else would ever dare to say in polite company," the duke said, shaking his head. "I am sure your mother was sufficiently shocked."

Lord Hemingway smiled as he took a sip of his own drink, rocking back and forth on his heels. "I've always enjoyed Lady Winchester, actually."

"Many do," the duke said, "as long as you are not on the receiving end of her barbs."

"I see my mother is speaking to Lady Bennington. The poor woman."

"Yes," the duke said diplomatically. "Lady Maria's disappearance has been quite the shock."

"Lady Dennison, you mean," Lord Hemingway said, and the duke nodded.

"Of course. My apologies."

"None taken by me," Hemingway said. "In fact, I rather wish she had remained Lady Maria."

"Oh?" the duke asked with some surprise.

"Yes. After you turned her down, I should have made my interest clear," Hemingway said with a sigh. "Of course, there was that whole business with Lady Juliana, unfortunately."

His eyes flashed slightly at that, and Hudson recalled that Hemingway had been expected to marry the duke's sister, but she had fallen in love with the detective instead. He couldn't imagine that her decision had been met with much acceptance from either family.

"Sorry about that whole business," the duke said, slapping a hand on Hemingway's shoulder. "You know Juliana. Always does the opposite of what everyone expects."

"Yes," Hemingway said, his eyes darkening, and Hudson sensed an edge to Hemingway's demeanor. Should Juliana have something to fear from the man? The duke didn't seem concerned, although Hudson was aware that he considered the man one of his closest friends, so perhaps he could never hold such suspicions. He could imagine that the detective had looked into him, especially when they had both been interested in the same woman. Whether or not he had shared any of that information with the duke was another question.

"I hadn't realized that you were interested in Lady Maria," the duke said nonchalantly, with a quick glance at Hudson, who kept his face as neutral as he possibly could.

"She's a beautiful woman, and would make the perfect wife," Hemingway said, some longing on his face now. "But she had always been meant for you and then after you married Lady Emma, I thought I would give it some time. I suppose in the end, it was too *much* time."

Hudson found himself tensing at the man's words. For she would not have been the perfect wife for Hemingway — she would be the perfect wife for *him*.

Except, of course, that she was now married to another.

The jealousy that stormed inside of him scared him, even though he had no rational reason for it. As much as he wanted to leave this blasted ball where he didn't belong in order to return to her side, she could never be truly his.

He was not even entirely sure that she would want to spend the rest of her life with him, even if she had the option to do so. She was obviously attracted to him, had her own interest in being with him, but did she long for him with the intensity that he did for her? Or was it entirely one-sided?

Hudson ran a hand through his hair as he realized the duke was staring at him. He had been so lost in his thoughts that he had stopped following the conversation, although he didn't care any longer what Hemingway had to say. The man could long for Maria all he wanted — she was now out of his reach.

The longer he was here, the more he realized that the only thing that could keep him from wanting Maria even more than he already did was if she had no interest in the same from him.

And there was only one way to find that out.

* * *

MARIA SAT in the front room of the Smiths' home, looking out into the inky blackness of night. Hudson had said that he wouldn't be long, but Maria had been to enough of those events to know that they most often went long into the early hours of the morning.

The Smiths had offered her their bedroom, but Maria had refused to put them out. She told them she had no problem in staying awake, waiting for Hudson to return. She wondered what they thought of the entire affair but was grateful they didn't comment on it to her, as she had no idea how she would explain herself and the situation.

With her head elsewhere, she jumped when she saw a figure appear in the darkness in front of the door, although her heart slowed when she saw who it was.

"Hudson," she said, opening the door, unable to help the smile that bloomed across her face. She had always been taught to play the coy lady, to never reveal her true emotion or sentiments toward a man — or any person at all, for that matter. But she couldn't seem to help them from emerging when it came to Hudson.

He stepped through the door wordlessly, not even looking around to see if the Smiths were about before he wrapped his arms around her and pulled her in tightly against him. Maria pressed her face into his jacket, finding his true scent beneath the cloying perfumes and odors of food and drink that laid on top of it, ones she was all too familiar with.

He leaned back and placed a gentle kiss on her lips.

"Was it that bad?" she asked, wrinkling her nose at him.

"Terrible," he said. "But it is all worth it when I am returning home to you."

She smiled wider at that and stepped back away from him as Mr. Smith emerged from the bedroom and wished them goodnight. Hudson led Maria out the door, and together they headed toward what even Maria was beginning to consider as home.

CHAPTER 16

"Tell me about the evening," Maria said as Hudson opened the door to his house, taking his usual perusal to ensure nothing had been disturbed.

"It was… enlightening," Hudson said before returning to her. He took her hand and began walking her back to the bedroom, describing the evening's events and revelations as they went.

Maria knew she should be most concerned about her husband, but she couldn't help but focus on one person he had only briefly mentioned.

"My mother was there?"

"She was."

"Was she… upset?"

Hudson took off his cravat, folding it before placing it in his wardrobe. Maria had the impression he was trying to decide just what to say.

"I believe that she is quite worried; however, from what I could tell, she was hiding the truth of what she felt."

"That sounds like her," Maria said wryly, which was true.

Her mother had always taught her to hide her emotion because it was how she, in turn, had been raised.

"Your husband was another story entirely," Hudson said, pulling her close and beginning to remove the pins from her hair. She turned around, enjoying the intimacy.

"In what way?"

"He was acting as though he didn't have a wife. He was quite jovial, flirting, playing cards with other men. He left when I did, although I gather that he was likely continuing on elsewhere."

"Another establishment that would be far from reputable, I expect."

"Likely. Warwick is going to speak with Archibald about him as well as this Lord Trundelle. Do you know of him?"

"Somewhat. He is a rather reclusive sort, not one who often frequents such events, though his brother often does. I wonder why he was in attendance."

"A question for the duchess, I suppose. It was quite a large gathering, so perhaps the invitation was sent to any noble family currently in London."

"Likely," she said with a nod.

Hudson turned her around, his fingers coming below her chin, lifting her head to look at him.

"What's wrong?"

"How do you know that something is wrong?"

"I can sense it."

"It is my mother, and how to go forward. What to expect. What my life will look like. The same concerns — ones I cannot shake, as nothing will change them."

Hudson reached out and took her hands in his, joining their fingers together.

"This isn't a change, but there is something you should know."

Was he going to tell her that it was time for her to leave

his home? That they couldn't possibly have a life together, not with her already being married and him being unable to leave his life and practice? The thought was rational, understandable, and yet, she wasn't sure she would be able to take hearing those words. Her heart began to pound as she stared up into his eyes, somewhat comforted when the deep blue that stared back at her did not appear overly concerned.

"I love you."

Maria's eyes widened and she was sure her mouth dropped open slightly. "You... what?"

"I love you," he said with a shrug of his shoulders. "I believe I have since I met you. You are the kindest, gentlest, most wonderful woman I have ever met. If I hadn't allowed my pride to come between us, perhaps I could have told you this before you had married the earl. It might not have changed anything, but I should have taken the chance. I know now is likely too late, but whatever you decide for the future, Maria, I would like to be there with you. Loving you, supporting you, taking care of you."

Maria's eyes began to fill with tears, and she had to clear her throat as it became clogged with emotion.

"Oh, Hudson," she said, leaning into him. "I love you too. So much. I just... I feel that you deserve better than a woman who is on the run from her old life, who cannot provide you with her hand in truth. I love you and would love to have a family with you. But... while to me, they would be born in love and that is enough for me now, I know that you vowed to never have children with a woman without that certainty of a marriage behind them."

He dipped his head for a moment, and she knew that this part hadn't been easy for him, which she could understand wholeheartedly.

"I know, Maria, I do," he said, meeting her eyes again. "And while we wouldn't be wed in truth, I would be there for them, raising them. In their eyes, we would be husband and wife, as we would be in mine. I would never allow my children to grow up without a father as I did, and I would be twice the father that any other man could ever be to his children. I promise you that."

Maria launched herself into his arms then, knowing the truth of what he said, feeling guilty she wouldn't be able to give him what he truly wanted but knowing that she also couldn't say goodbye and let him go. How could she? If he loved her enough that he chose to be with her in turn, then she was his. For as long as he wanted her.

She lifted her face to his and he leaned down, taking her lips sweetly, gently, drinking her in, telling her now with his mouth as he had with his words what she meant to him, what they could be together. His hands drew around her back as hers lifted to wrap around the skin that was now bared to her around his neck, and she pressed herself close, needing more.

Maria could hardly believe she had married another man, that she would have had to subject herself to him when the man she had always wanted, needed, loved, was here with her now, in her arms, his touch as loving as his words.

Which, in the end, was the most important vow she could ever imagine.

She leaned back from him long enough for him to unfasten the back of her dress, which she let slide down her body before bending over and removing her boots, followed by her undergarments until she was bare before him. Not long ago she would have been utterly abashed to be so absolutely naked in front of him, but now she had no qualms, for she knew that Hudson loved her and accepted her, for all that she was.

Only now she was eager for him to be as exposed as she was, to feel his skin pressed against hers.

She pushed off the sleeves of his jacket, and he grinned, obviously enjoying her undressing him. Maria rather enjoyed it herself as she continued her quest, ridding him of his waist jacket next, followed by his linen shirt. He had to help her with that, sliding it over his head, for she couldn't quite reach high enough.

When he was disrobed from the waist up, she slid her hand down the muscles of his chest, enjoying herself as she did so, until she reached the waistband of his breeches. She knelt and began to unfasten them slowly, and then inched them down his legs. That was when he seemed to lose control, as he lifted her up, kicked off his boots and the remainder of his breeches, and laid her down on the bed before him.

"You," he said, leaning overtop of her, "are mine, Maria. It doesn't matter if you were married to that man in name. You are mine in body, in spirit, in heart. Do you understand?"

"I understand," she said, her heart pounding in her chest. Him speaking like this might have scared her when she had first come to him, but she knew him so well now, trusted him so intensely, that she relished the possessiveness he felt toward her.

"Say it," he commanded, and her eyes widened.

"Say what?"

"That you are mine."

"I am yours," she said, but then she couldn't help her lips from curling into a smile. "And you are mine."

He leaned over top of her, his strong arms framing her head. "I am yours."

He finally took her lips then, giving her satisfaction more delicious than any drink of chocolate or piece of cake could ever be.

Their tongues tangled in a ferocity she hadn't known to

expect, until Maria was overwhelmed with an urge to show him just what he meant to her.

She saw the surprise on his face when she wiggled from underneath him and pressed his shoulder back until he was the one lying beneath her. His lips curled into a satisfied grin — but she wasn't finished yet. She leaned down and experimented by kissing his neck, then continuing downward over his chest. She looked up to see if he was enjoying what she was doing, and when she found that his eyes were half-hooded and heavy as he stared at her, she decided that she would continue.

Maria let her tongue travel over the muscles of his stomach, heady with the power that surged through her as she set her hands around his hips. When she reached his cock, straining toward her, she leaned down and wrapped her lips around the very tip of it, causing Hudson to groan and wrap his hands around the back of her head, twining his fingers into her hair as he gently moved her head back and forth and she used her tongue as she had last time.

"Maria," he said, his voice sounding pained, and she gripped the base of him with her other hand as she continued to move her mouth as though she was kissing his lips. She looked up and met his eyes, noting how hard he was breathing, until he leaned down and reached his fingers underneath her chin, gently tugging her toward him.

"Maria," he said again, only this time much firmer. "Come here."

He laid her on the bed, anticipation in his smile before he dipped down below her waist as she had done him.

He grinned predatorily at her as he copied what she had done to him, grasping her hips and then leaning his head to her thighs, running his teeth along the inside of them as he came dangerously close to her — danger that she was beginning to welcome.

"I'm going to taste you," he said, and an ache throbbed between Maria's thighs, growing more desperate the closer he came as he used his tongue and his teeth to draw near to her. Finally, his tongue reached her center, and when he found her bundle of nerves, she let out a moan, grateful that Hudson lived somewhere that she didn't have to worry about neighbors hearing her cries.

His tongue worked her up and down as she had to grab onto the sheets in order to keep from flying off the bed as her hips began rocking along with him. Maria wasn't sure that she had ever felt anything better in her entire life — until he stopped abruptly, leaning up over top of her, his grin still apparent.

"What do you want, Maria?"

"I want you."

"In what way?" he asked, and she eyed him, shaking her head, too shy to say it aloud.

"Hudson…"

"I want to hear the words on your tongue," he said again, and she closed her eyes, both completely hungry for him while also completely mortified.

"Please, Hudson, I want you… inside of me."

He held himself over top of her, lowering his hips so that he was just in front of her entrance.

"What the lady wants, the lady gets," he said, pushing himself in with one solid thrust, and Maria let out another long moan at how complete he made her feel. This time there was no need for him to be slow or gentle, and he began to rock in and out of her faster, harder, and Maria wrapped her legs around him, pulling him as close as she could.

"Hudson," she said, reaching up a hand toward him. "That feels… amazing."

He continued, perspiration breaking out on his brow as he thrust in and out of her, the muscles of his stomach rippling with his movements, and Maria didn't think she had ever seen anything more glorious in her life. If this is what she had to look forward to for the rest of her years, then she was happy to do whatever it took to make it so.

He stopped suddenly, his chest heaving, and he pulled out of her, causing her to cry out in dismay.

"Turn over," he said, and she was powerless to do anything but listen to his commands, doing as he said before he helped her to her knees.

"Bend your chest down, but keep your hips up," he ordered. "But Maria, if this is too much, if you want me to stop, just say the word."

She nodded and waited as he pushed himself in once more and she gasped at the difference this angle made. He began to move again, and she thought she might come apart right then.

"Does that feel all right?" he asked.

"Yes," she gasped, unable to say anything further.

"Maria..." he said, his breath as desperate as hers. "I love how you feel around me. You are... everything. You are... perfect."

He continued to pound harder, until all of Maria's thoughts fled except for those that included Hudson and his body, moving in and out of her, working her into a state of near madness.

Just when Maria wasn't sure that she could take any more, he pulled out of her and turned her to her back once more.

"I need to see your face," he said, as he leaned over her and thrust in again. He dipped his head, kissing her, and as he moved with his body and his lips, Maria began to come apart. She could feel the rush building from within her, as it had before, only this time it was different, harder, deeper, and then Hudson finally stopped as he clutched his arms around her, shuddering with his own release as the waves of pleasure continued to pulse through Maria.

When it all subsided for both of them, Hudson leaned up on his fists, staring down at her with such intensity that it didn't seem like words would be enough, which he solved by leaning in and taking her lips with his once more. She wrapped her arms around him as they told each other all they needed to with their kisses, their tongues, their lips.

Finally, he rolled beside her, though he kept his arms around her and held her close.

"I love you," he whispered, kissing her temple.

"I love you, too."

And she would do anything — *anything* — to protect that love.

CHAPTER 17

*H*udson stared at Maria the next morning. She looked so peaceful sleeping in his bed, her blond curls laid out around her head like a halo.

He had just answered a knock at his door, already called to see his first patient before he could wake slowly to begin his day and his usual round of house calls.

Now he was torn. Did he wake Maria and insist she accompany him, or did he let her sleep? He wondered if his lovemaking had been too much for her last night, although from what he could tell, she had seemed to enjoy it. Now he was feeling somewhat guilty, although from the way the corners of her lips were slightly turned up, even in sleep, he had a feeling that she had enjoyed it as much as he had.

Finally, he decided that since he was only going down the street, she would be fine. No one was going to try anything in the early hours of the morning. Dennison was the threat they were most concerned about, and the man likely was just going to bed at this point, not awakening to determine the whereabouts of his wife.

Hudson found his quill pen and inkwell, scratched a

quick note on a piece of paper that he left next to the tea kettle, and then slipped out. It should just be a quick assessment, and then he would be home, back with Maria once more.

He locked the door behind him as he started down the cobblestones, whistling a tune as he went. He had a practice that helped people in his community and beyond, and a woman he loved beyond belief — a woman he would never have imagined would ever feel anything toward him, but who, inexplicably, loved him as he did her.

When he reached the Coopers' door, he pushed the thoughts away in order to focus on the task at hand. Then, when he finished, he could go back to his dreaming once more.

* * *

MARIA WOKE in a haze of happiness.

The smile was on her face before she even opened her eyes.

Hudson loved her. He had told her, he had shown her, and he had vowed to always be there for her. He made her feel indescribable sensations and emotions that she hadn't even known were possible. Now she understood Juliana's small smiles when she spoke of her husband and the happiness they had found together.

When she looked over to find that Hudson's place in the bed was empty, she walked out to the main room, expecting him to be sitting there with two cups of tea. Instead, she was greeted with a note saying that he had gone out, but the kettle was ready for her to prepare her own tea. She dressed as she waited for it to heat, appreciating that these garments allowed her to dress herself without the assistance of a maid, as Hudson's wouldn't arrive for another hour.

When the tea was ready, she wrapped her hands around the warmth of the mug before walking to the window to look out at the neighborhood beyond.

She was still becoming used to the fact that this part of London was so alive at this hour of the day. In Mayfair, there would be servants and merchants about, but otherwise the residents preferred to sleep until a much later hour. Here, residents lived by the light.

She sniffed the air, wondering if a baker had overcooked the bread this morning as she sensed a note of burning, but then jumped when a knock sounded at the door.

Maria frowned, wondering who it could possibly be. Most likely it was a patient seeking Hudson. Should she answer it? She placed her tea down and decided that as the physician's assistant, she could have reason for being here during the day. A small warning tugged at her that it might not be completely safe to answer, but she told herself that Lord Dennison would never come after her at this hour of the morning.

"Miss? Where is the physician?"

A boy stood before her, one who worked for his own coin in the street from the looks of him. He had likely been sent by a patient to fetch Hudson.

"He left on another call, but I expect him back shortly," she said. "Why do you not tell me where he is needed, and I will be sure to send him on his way when he returns?"

"It's not that," he said with a shake of his head, and she noticed then that he was rocking back and forth from one foot to the other in agitation. "It's the house."

"What house?"

"This house."

"I apologize, but I am not sure what you mean."

"There's a fire out back," he finally managed, and it took Maria a moment to understand what he was saying.

"What?"

"Come, miss!" he said, and as Maria followed him out the door, she realized that she could possibly be walking into a trap — what were the odds that this would happen while Hudson was out? — but she couldn't very well stay in a house that someone claimed was on fire, now could she?

As she stepped out the front door, however, she could smell the smoke in the air immediately, and she and the boy increased their pace as he led her around the back of the building, where she could see grey smoke now drifting through the street.

Maria let out a gasp as she saw that flames had taken over a pile of food waste behind the house while flames were licking the brick through a broken window — one that she knew led into Hudson's study.

"Oh no!" she cried, as she was already running back to the house. She had to return and try to take whichever implements she could. She knew how important it all was to him, and how much it had cost him to build his inventory of tools. If he lost them all, he could very well lose his practice.

She heard the boy cry out behind her, "Miss!" even as men began to run toward the building.

"Call the Fire Brigade!" she heard someone shout behind her, while another voice called out, "which one?"

Good heavens, if they didn't even know who to call yet, the building was under dire threat of being lost. The small townhouse had a brick façade, but if the fire was both inside and out, it was unlikely it all could be saved, was it not? Maria had never seen a fire firsthand, but she had heard enough about devastating fires which destroyed everything in their path. She could only pray that wouldn't be the case for all that Hudson had built.

How could it possibly have started, she wondered as she pushed open the door of the house. She hadn't even entered the study this morning and she could hardly see Hudson leaving a lit candle within. As she opened the door and looked to the back room, however, her heart leapt into her throat, for she could see that the flames were already surging forward, having engulfed the room. There was no way that she could possibly save Hudson's tools, and it seemed unlikely that his home would even withstand the blaze.

She let out a cry of frustration as she turned to go, realizing that all she could do now was save herself. As she was about to take a step out the door, however, something caught her eye.

It was so small she barely noticed it, but it seemed out of place in the middle of Hudson's well-kept rooms.

She bent, picking up the small piece of jewellery — and her breath caught when she recognized the crest that was engraved in the red stone.

It was the Dennison crest.

He had been here. She was sure of it, down to her very bones. He knew where she was and was coming after her. Whether he had meant for her to be caught in the fire or not, she had no idea, but she wasn't going to give him the satisfaction of having trapped her.

As she burst through the door, she caught a glimpse of Hudson running down the street at full speed. He had lost his cap in his race, and she could only hope that his patient had been well when he left. She picked up her skirts and began her own run toward him. When she drew closer, he dropped his bag to the ground and reached out to catch her in his arms.

* * *

HUDSON HAD JUST FINISHED his consultation when the door of the Coopers' home had burst open to reveal a woman shouting that his house was on fire. It had taken him a moment to realize what she was saying, and when he did, his heart had leapt in his throat.

Maria.

He had left without a word, praying as he ran out the door that she had been able to get out in time, or if not, that the fire brigade had arrived in time to help her escape. They had to. For he could not lose her. Not now. Not like this.

He was a few blocks away and ran down the street faster than he could ever remember doing so in his life.

He didn't register people shouting his name as he went by, nor the rumble of the fire engine as the brigade seemed to be coming. As he began to near his house, the first thing he saw was his neighbors — people he had come to know as patients, as friends, working diligently, passing one another buckets of water to try to douse the flames. From the size of the fire that he could see, he doubted that their efforts would make much difference, but he appreciated it all the same.

Then, thank goodness, he saw her.

She emerged from the building with tendrils of smoke curling behind her, and she turned one way and then the next until she caught sight of him and began running toward him. They met in the middle of the street, and he couldn't stop himself from lifting her in his arms, holding her tightly against him as he waited a moment for the relief to rush through him.

"Thank God you are safe," he said, leaning back now to take a closer look at her. "You are not injured? You did not breathe in smoke?"

"No," she shook her head, her hair still down around her shoulders, although she was dressed for the day. "I didn't even know a fire had started until a boy knocked on the door. It seemed to have begun in the study. I tried to get out all of your implements, Hudson, but by the time I got there, the entire room was engulfed and—"

He lifted a finger in front of her lips.

"Maria. It doesn't matter what was in there. All that is important is that you are out safely."

"But all that you worked for, it was all—"

"Most of what I worked for is up here," he said, tapping a finger against the side of his head. "Instruments can be replaced. But you cannot be."

Now that his relief at seeing her had filled him, Hudson began to try to think back as to whether or not he had left anything aflame in the room. He certainly couldn't recall doing so, although how else could such a fire begin?

Maria was wringing her hands together nervously, and he drew her back away from the building as he watched the fire brigade go to work. He was glad he had paid for insurance, although it was obvious that much would be lost. The insurance would cover the structure, although Maria was right about one thing — he had lost everything within. He would just have to build it back up, he supposed.

"I wonder if this is a sign," he mused aloud.

"A sign?" Maria asked, turning to him.

"That we should leave. Find somewhere else to live, where no one knows who we are. We could start anew. I can begin my practice once more."

Melancholy settled over him as he said it, and he wasn't sure why — until he noticed the people who had begun to gather around him.

Smith came over to him first, laying a hand on his shoulder.

"I'm sorry," was all he said, as Mrs. Smith came over to speak to Maria.

All of the people were out now — the Bloomsburys, the Coopers, everyone he had grown to know and love. This was what it meant to be part of a community, a neighborhood, a family.

"I don't know, Hudson," Maria murmured as she looked around. "The people here love you. You are one of them. They need you."

He turned toward her now, placing an arm around her as he drew her in close. "I need you more."

She nodded slightly, but she seemed troubled, and he could imagine why. She had left one terrible situation in which she was threatened only for the home she had begun to live in to be burned to the ground — for he had an inkling that was what was going to happen. At least it appeared that the homes and businesses near him were not going to suffer the same fate. He would feel ever responsible if something happened to his neighbours and friends.

Now that the fire brigade had arrived with their pump, the men of the neighborhood had stopped their attempts to douse the fire. Instead, they all stood next to him in solidarity.

And as he held Maria close to him, he wondered just what they were going to do next.

CHAPTER 18

*M*aria stood woodenly by Hudson's side as they watched his home burn.

Because the walls were made of brick, it appeared they were actually able to save much of the exterior, but she could only imagine what it looked like within.

She was fiddling with the ring in her pocket, wondering just what she was supposed to do with it and the information it provided, when she felt a tug on her dress, on the side that was away from Hudson. She glanced over at him, but he was busy talking to Mr. Smith and didn't notice.

"Yes?" she said, turning to the boy — a different one than who had knocked on her door.

"I was asked to give this to ya," he said, passing her a small slip of paper, one that appeared of rather fine quality, and she took it with some consternation. She stayed turned to the side as she read it, her heart leaping into her throat as she did.

"What's wrong?"

She turned to find Hudson looking at her with worry.

How did he always seem to know when something was amiss?

"Nothing," she managed. "It is just so awful that you have lost so much."

"I told you. It could have been far worse," he said, squeezing her hand as he smiled at her, although she knew the expression was rather forced, which made sense after all that had occurred.

She bit her lip as the words from the paper danced around in her mind.

You can run all you want, wife, but I will find you. The doctor escaped the morgue this time, but he shall be there soon enough — and I will claim what is mine.

Maria swallowed hard as she blinked back tears. She had been so afraid for her own life that she had never stopped to consider what protecting her could mean for Hudson. He was not distraught over the destruction of his house, which she understood, but what if it had been his life? What if he had been killed in a fire because he had taken her in, loved her, provided for her? He had vowed to her that he would do anything to protect her, and while she hadn't used the words, she would most certainly do the same for him. She could never forgive herself if he was injured — or worse — because of her.

But what did that mean for them now? She looked up at his beautiful profile as he gazed at the building that had been both his home and his business. She thought of his mother, who had devoted her entire life to ensure that Hudson had been able to build one that was worthy of what she had wanted for him, for a duke's son, bastard that he may be.

Could she ask him to leave it all behind? Or did she have to make the unthinkable decision to leave on her own, if it meant that he would live the life he was supposed to while staying safe? The thought nearly wrenched her in two, but before she could dwell on it any longer, a voice, loud and insistent, rent through the air and tore her from her disturbing thoughts.

"Hudson!"

They turned in unison to see Hudson's mother come running down the street.

"Oh, dear," Hudson murmured. "Brace yourself."

"Hudson!" She shouted again, and this time Maria didn't miss the man who was accompanying her, doing his best to keep up even though he was clearly struggling, being rather portly, although his effort was valiant. She finally reached them, her hands extending to cup Hudson's cheeks. "Are you well? What happened? Oh, your house. Everything you worked so hard for. Up in flames! I could hardly believe it when I heard. I didn't believe it, actually. I had to come see for myself. We just returned and then I heard shouts through the streets that the physician's home was aflame, that all were to watch for their own homes. How *devastating*."

"Mother," Hudson finally managed when she paused to take a breath. "I am fine. The house will need considerable repair, 'tis true, but no one was injured and the fire will not spread."

"But how did this happen?" his mother asked, her eyes flitting to the side to take in Maria, and Maria couldn't help but bristle slightly at the accusation in her stare.

"We don't know yet," Hudson said. "I am sure we will discover that in the coming days. The fire began behind the house and in my study."

"Where you kept everything?" His mother said, and it looked to Maria like she was about to weep.

"Yes," he said calmly. "But it can all be replaced. I was out on a call, and Maria managed to leave in time."

His mother turned to her now, fixing her full attention on her.

"Did you light a candle in there?"

Maria's mouth dropped open as she shook her head. "No, I had not entered the room prior to the fire. I—"

She was about to say she had just awoken, but she was unsure what Hudson's mother would think of their continued living arrangements.

"Maria had nothing to do with the fire, Mother," Hudson said, a bit more impatiently now. "Why do we not allow the fire brigade to continue their work? Do you mind if we come to your place, Mother? I will spread the word that I can be found there should anyone need me."

"Of course," she said, slightly mollified now. Hudson then finally noticed the man standing next to his mother. Having finally recovered his breath, he nodded at Hudson.

"We have not yet met," he said, holding out a hand. "I am Sir Willoughby."

"Sir Willoughby?" Hudson said, raising his eyes as he took the man's hand. "It is... good to meet you."

Maria could see the question in his stare, but he didn't say anything as the four of them began the short walk to his mother's house after Hudson retrieved his bag from where he had dropped it. It seemed odd, to be walking without any of her possessions, but then, nothing within Hudson's home was really hers, now was it? She asked about his gig, but he told her the stables were as close to his mother's home as his own.

"Tell me, Maria," Hudson's mother said as they walked, "what are you doing with my son?"

Maria cleared her throat, looking to Hudson, who nodded at her.

"Well, you know that I escaped a... situation."

"I do."

"I was injured."

"Are you well now?"

149

"I am, thank you," Maria said with a small smile. As intimidated as she was by Hudson's mother, she had a feeling that beneath her bluster, the woman was truly simply trying to protect her son. "Dr. Lewis has been most generous with his time to ensure that I am well."

"I'm sure he has," his mother said with a look over at her son. "And now what will you do?"

"Mother," Hudson interjected, "Now is not the time for this discussion."

"Is it not?" she asked, raising a brow as she placed her hands on her hips. "Maria is coming to stay at my house. I should know in what capacity I am to welcome her."

"I love her," Hudson said quietly. "That is all you need to know for now. The situation is complicated, but we will determine a way forward together."

"I see," his mother said, and while she obviously didn't see at all, she must have sensed Hudson's disinterest in talking about it any further, for which Maria was grateful.

While the conversation had been uncomfortable, perhaps it was necessary — for it reminded Maria of the truth.

They did not have an easy path forward here in Holborn, where everyone knew them. They could not be married, and they could not build a life together living in sin. Even his mother likely wouldn't accept it — certainly not forever.

Maria was going to have to make a decision. And she was going to have to make it soon — for they were already in far too deep.

* * *

HUDSON WAS SURPRISED to find his mother's house empty when he returned home after his rounds, and he sat back on the sofa with a sigh. What a day it had been. While he had been dealing with trying to make himself and Maria comfortable at his mother's small home, he had still made sure to complete his calls and see all who came for his help — it hadn't taken long for anyone to locate him. Word spread fast in this neighborhood.

Generosity spread quickly as well. In no time, his mother's home was filled with more food than they could ever eat before it began to rot, as everyone attempted to help the physician in some way.

He had only lived here a few short years and already, he could hardly imagine leaving this neighborhood and the people within it.

His mother, fortunately, had an extra bedroom, where Hudson had insisted Maria stay. He assumed she was now asleep after the ordeal of this morning. His mother was dining at Sir Willoughby's. He had asked that she stay and look after Maria until he finished his calls, but she told him she would be leaving not long before he arrived home, so Maria would only be alone for a short time. Hudson had seen to his patients alone, not wanting to ask Maria to accompany him when she'd already had enough commotion in one day. He had been concerned about the drawn, worried look on her face and decided the last thing she needed was to add ill, upset patients to her list of troubles.

After finishing his drink, however, he found that he needed her, craved her presence. Even if she was asleep, he decided, his mother wasn't home so why could he not enter her bedroom and lie down next to her? Just small contact with her was enough to keep him satisfied — for now, at least.

He pushed open the bedroom door, a smile on his lips, for despite the fact he had lost much of what he had built today, he had Maria — and that was what truly mattered. The rest could be restored.

But the smile fell when he found the bed empty. There

was a slight indentation in the blankets covering the mattress, telling him that she had been lying upon it at one point in time, but otherwise the room had been deserted, with only a hint of her scent still wafting through the air.

His heart began racing in panic as his first thought was that she had been taken against her will, but the door had been locked when he arrived, and there was no sign of struggle or forced entry. Perhaps she had left to the market, he reasoned. Although, as she always refused to take any payment, she had very little coin, unless his mother had left some for her.

His mother. He would go ask her if she knew of anything amiss. Perhaps Maria had accompanied her to Sir Willoughby's. He wasn't entirely sure where the man lived, but he emerged from her house, asking a few neighbors until he was provided an answer. It wasn't far, near to Leicester Square, and he knocked loudly on the door, knowing he was likely being rude but too desperate for answers to care.

A servant answered the door and Hudson made his request to see his mother as calmly as he could. His mother emerged into the foyer, dressed much finer than he had ever seen her before. Hudson started slightly, knowing there was obviously much more going on here than he had guessed, but now was not the time for questions regarding her relationship with Sir Willoughby.

"Hudson? What is it?"

"Mother, where is Maria?"

His mother frowned. "At my house, where I left her not long ago."

"She's not there."

"What do you mean?"

"She's gone," Hudson said, trying to keep his tone even, although he couldn't help the desperate panic that filled him. "I returned from my call, and she wasn't there. No sign of her except an indent on the bed. Did she say anything to you about where she was going?"

"Nothing," his mother said, shaking her head, her forehead now creased in worry. "Hudson."

He was already turning to the door, trying to decide where to look next, but he stopped to listen to his mother.

"Yes?"

"Do you think perhaps... she thought it best to leave?"

"What do you mean?"

"I know some of her story and she could have realized that by staying she was only making a complicated situation even worse."

Hudson released the door handle to turn toward his mother, walking closer toward her. "I love her, and she loves me. We are building a life together, and that is all that matters. Nothing else."

"But if that life you want to build is in jeopardy, as it appeared today..."

All of the blood drained from Hudson's face as he brought a hand to his head. While he wanted to tell his mother that she was wrong, that it would never be the case, that they could withstand all that came at them, came for him, what she said made some sense.

What if Maria had worried that the fire was because of her and had decided that the only option for her was to leave? But where would she go? What would she do? And could she be in danger of Dennison finding her?

"I have to go, Mother," he said, and she opened her mouth, but he shook his head. "Enjoy your dinner. I will return to your home to tell you what is happening."

She finally nodded, and before he could leave, she leaned in impulsively and placed a kiss on his cheek.

"I only want what is best for you, son," she said fiercely. "I always have."

"I know, Mother," he said. "And you have done so all your life. But now it is time for me to decide what is best for me, while you live the life you deserve. Do you understand?"

She nodded. "I do."

"Goodnight, then."

And with that, he was out the door, off to find the woman he loved. To start, he was going to need some help.

CHAPTER 19

*A*dded to the rest of her sins, now Maria was a thief.

She had found some spare coin in Hudson's mother's house and had taken it, although she had left a note in its place, promising that when she was able to earn coin of her own, she would return it.

How she would do so, she had no idea, but she supposed that was a problem for another day. For today, she just had to get away. The farther she ran from Hudson, the safer he would be.

Even though she had left her heart behind with him.

She thought of going to Juliana, for she knew she would help her, but she also knew that Juliana would try to convince her to stay — and she would likely succeed. Which would only lead to further heartbreak later on, for both Maria and Hudson.

When she thought of who else she could turn to, who would keep her secret and help her, only one other person came to mind — Lady Winchester.

She used her stolen coin to hire a hack to convey her to Mayfair, and once there she used the remainder to pay a boy to go to the servants' entrance and relay her note to Lady Winchester's lady's maid. She had a fair amount of time to wait outside the iron fence that separated the duke's grand mansion from the rest of London, but soon enough, Lady Winchester emerged.

Maria escaped from the shadows to wave to her, and Lady Winchester ambled over and took a seat on the bench next to her, as she had but a short time ago at a different Mayfair address.

"I thought I told you that I did not want to see you again, and yet, here we are once more," Lady Winchester began, although her words were said in kindness.

"You did, and you were right," Maria said, clutching her skirts in her hands, aware that this was the only clothing she had left in her name — and even this had been gifted. "Remaining with Hudson — that is, Dr. Lewis — has only placed him in danger as well."

"You're too close," Lady Winchester said, pursing her lips and shaking her head. "You need to place enough distance between you and Lord Dennison that he no longer puts in the effort to find you. He has eyes about London, and knowing you are here, with another man no less, is like waving a flag in front of a bull."

"I know," Maria said, dropping her head. "I was too cowardly, too selfish to go. But I have learned my lesson, and I will leave before it's too late."

"You need money, do you not?"

Maria nodded grimly, wiping away the tear that began to trickle from one of her eyes. "I hate to ask you, Lady Winchester, I do, but I did not know who else to turn to. I will repay it once I am able to earn something of my own. I promise you that."

"There is no need," Lady Winchester said, shaking her head again decisively. "When I received your note, I figured as much, and have brought you what I could. Unfortunately, I have no access to my grandson's fortune, but this should get you where you need to go. And take this."

She held out a sapphire broach that glinted in the light, and Maria was already shaking her head before she could look closer at it.

"I couldn't take that, Lady Winchester, although I am most appreciative of the offer."

"Nonsense. I have so many baubles that I scarcely ever wear. No one will miss it, and my granddaughters will have more than enough left to them already. Take it, and when you are able to sell it, be sure to receive back its value, do you understand?"

"I do," Maria said as the tears began falling at both the woman's generosity and her own grief at leaving Hudson behind.

"I do not like the thought of you out there all alone," Lady Winchester said, shaking her head curtly. "Have you asked him to accompany you?"

"Who, Dr. Lewis?" Maria asked, her eyes widening.

"Of course."

"No," Maria shook her head. "I could not ask him to come with me. His life is here. His profession. His mother."

"Should it not be his choice?"

"If I put the choice before him, he would feel obligated to come with me, when that would not be what he wanted. I cannot put him in such a position."

"Very well," Lady Winchester said with a sigh. "I am sorry you are in this predicament. I hope that you are able to find happiness elsewhere."

"Thank you," Maria said. "Thank you so much, Lady Winchester. For everything. If you do see Dr. Lewis... can you please tell him that I did this *because* I love him?"

"I should hope that he could ascertain that for himself."

Maria managed a watery smile and a nod of her head before standing, picking up her skirts, and making her way to find another hack. She had a new destination, and she was going to have to hurry.

* * *

"What do you mean she is *gone?*"

Juliana stared at Hudson in shock, appearing rather frightening with the flash in her eyes as she stared him down, making him feel that he was the one responsible for Maria's disappearance. Which in a sense, he supposed he was, for he hadn't done as he promised — kept her safe, provided her every reason to trust him with anything that threatened her. At Juliana's ire, one of her cats stalked toward him with eyes similarly glinting, and he took a step backward until Juliana stopped it.

"I was on a call, and when I returned to my mother's house, she had left."

"Where was your mother?"

"At a dinner."

"You left Maria alone?"

"Juliana, she had been through quite an ordeal. I didn't see fit to drag her around London seeing patients, and I thought she would be safe at Mother's. In fact, I'm *sure* she was safe there, but for some reason, she decided to leave of her own accord."

"I don't understand."

"All I need to know is whether or not she came here to you."

"No, she didn't. Of course I would tell you if she had."

Hudson was raking his hands through his hair just as the door opened to reveal Archibald.

"Lewis," he said with a nod as the dogs jumped upon him in excited greeting. "I was looking for you."

"Why, have you seen Maria?"

"Maria? No. It's about your house. After the fire brigade left, we took a look ourselves, and soon realized the fire was set deliberately. I am sure the brigade will determine the same."

Hudson sank into a chair. Was someone trying to do away with Maria? Could this be tied to Dennison? And could all have been a way to force her out of the house so that they could access her elsewhere?

"What is this about Lady Maria?" Archibald asked now, crossing his arms over his chest as he looked from one of them to the other.

"Hudson lost her," Juliana said unhelpfully, and Hudson lowered his hands to glare at her. He liked his half-sister, but in times like these, she could be slightly grating as she didn't seem to understand the tact required.

"She is not a dog, Juliana. I believe she left of her own accord."

Archibald nodded knowingly. "Perhaps she somehow determined that she was the cause of the fire. She likely left to keep you safe."

"Keep *me* safe?" he said in disbelief. "That is what I was trying to do for her!"

"It is still possible for a woman to look after a man in her own way," Juliana said with a slight eyeroll.

"I know, Juliana, I do, I just… why wouldn't she tell me?"

"Would you have stopped her?" Juliana asked.

"Of course I would have."

"Then that is why she didn't. Likely the same reason why she didn't come here to me for help."

"We need to find her before Dennison does." Hudson said,

standing and beginning to pace back and forth through the small room.

"Do you think he knows she has left?" Juliana asked, and Archibald stepped in.

"It's a possibility. If he knew where she was, which it seems he did, then it is likely he had a man keeping an eye on her. He might not have heard word yet, but he could soon. I agree that we need to hurry."

Hudson didn't like the sounds of that.

"We need help," he said, and Archibald nodded.

"I can ask my men to be on the lookout."

"And we should go to Giles," Juliana said, though she hadn't finished speaking when Hudson was already shaking his head.

"He doesn't need to be involved."

"He does. He would want to be. So would Emma and Prudence. I shall go tell them what is happening."

"No," Archibald said swiftly. "If a threat is still possible to either Maria or to the family, you should not be wandering alone. Hell, Dennison could be the one behind everything, based on what Lewis and the duke overheard."

"Speaking of that, did you find anything out?" Hudson asked. It would solve a lot of his problems if Dennison was sent to the gallows, although it was not a likely outcome for a high-ranking peer.

"Now is not the time for full details, but yes, it seems that Dennison and Trundelle owe the former duke a great amount of money. Somehow the vowels have been lost, but the duke is determining what has become of them. For now, however, we need to find Maria. I will summon my men and have one of them send a note round to Warwick House. We should meet here so as to not raise any suspicions in Mayfair."

"Very well," Hudson said. "What should I do in the meantime?"

"Wait."

"Wait?" he cried. "Hardly."

"Better than you running around London for us to come find you as well," Archibald said. "I will not be long. Then we will formulate a plan that will have us finding her in a hurry. I am assuming she doesn't have much to spend so she cannot have gone far. If she is planning to leave London, then someone must have helped her. Once we determine who that is, we can narrow things down."

He left then, and Hudson looked to Juliana in some supplication. She seemed to understand what he was feeling, for she came over to him and placed a hand on his arm.

"It will be all right."

"Will it though?"

"I suppose I cannot say that for sure. But we are all with you in this, and together we will find her. I feel it."

"What if…" he hadn't wanted to voice the thought aloud, but he felt that Juliana would understand. "What if she doesn't want to come back to me? What if she was running not just from Dennison, but from me as well? I thought she was happy with me, but perhaps I pushed her too hard, was too overbearing for her, asked too much of her."

"Is that what you truly think?" Juliana asked, looking him in the eye, and he sighed.

"It's what I fear."

"Do not let your fears overtake you. Ask yourself instead what you believe is the truth, deep inside. Trust your instinct, not what is scaring you. Listen to that voice instead."

He nodded, closing his eyes as he tried to decide what Maria would be feeling. From all he was aware, she loved him as much as he did her.

"You've figured it out, have you?" Juliana asked when he opened his eyes.

"She must have left because she thought it would be best for me," he said. "She was wrong, of course."

"Of course," Juliana agreed. "Now you have to find her and convince her of the fact."

If only that was as easy as she made it sound.

CHAPTER 20

*B*y the time Maria reached the docks, she was beginning to despair. She was aware that it was long past the dinner hour, and she was starving. In fact, she also felt slightly queasy, although she wasn't entirely sure why.

A sense of unease stole over her, and she glanced over her shoulder, knowing her suspicions were all from wondering whether she had made the right decision. It had seemed like she should do all she could to keep Hudson safe, and yet, leaving anywhere without him felt so wrong. What had been the point of it all? Of staying with him, of working for him, of falling in love with him? For here she was, exactly where she had started, only this time, her heart was breaking.

She disembarked from the hack as she kept her head down while trying to determine where to go. She had certainly never been taught in her upbringing how to secure passage on a ship. She looked for women to ask, although most eyed her suspiciously. When she did reach out, no one seemed to have an answer for her, and then before she could ask the next, she was suddenly overwhelmed by all that had happened, and she found herself leaning over the rail to be sick into the Thames below her.

When she rose again, she saw that she was receiving a fair number of stares, as darkness was beginning to creep over the horizon. There would certainly be no berths to be found today, and besides that, she had no idea where she was going anyway.

She best use some of her precious coin to find a place to sleep for the night, she considered. She would have to find an inn, although how to find a reputable one, she had no idea. She began walking down Thames Street, looking for some sign that would tell her which inn was one she could potentially trust.

She finally found one that appeared to be a coaching inn, and she followed a family inside. When she spoke to the proprietor, he eyed her suspiciously, but allowed her to pay for a room, with the promise that there would be "no visitors."

She readily agreed, for who would she want in a room with her other than Hudson? He told her dinner was available first, pointing to the tavern beyond and she nodded dejectedly as she took hesitant steps within and took a seat at a table, alone.

Maria glumly looked around the inn's tavern. How far one could fall in a short amount of time, she considered as she took in the scarred tables, the freely flowing drink, and the barely edible meals that were set before people around her. She supposed that was what would be placed in front of her shortly.

Was it truly only several weeks ago that she had been living a life of luxury that almost any woman in England would given all that she had for? Then she had sunk so low that she had married a husband she had to run from before he caused her a life of pain or worse, only to enter the arms of a man who took her to heights of love and pleasure that she had never known existed.

And now here she was — alone, with hardly a penny to her name, uncertain of her future and without the man she loved.

A woman walked over and shoved a plate underneath Maria's nose, jolting her from her musings. She looked down at the blobs of white that appeared to possibly be potatoes, and the meat that she couldn't have identified if she tried. She thought the small brown circles swimming in cream could be peas, but it was difficult to tell.

Then the scent hit her nose and she turned to the side as she gagged, nearly losing all the contents that remained in her stomach.

"You gonna be sick?"

Maria looked up to see a woman from a table next to her staring at her with some sympathy. She took a deep breath — away from the food's aroma — and her stomach slightly settled.

"I believe I shall be fine."

"Good. Ya carrying or something?"

"Carrying?" Maria asked, wrinkling her nose.

"With child, luv."

The man across from the woman, who appeared to be her husband, shook his head at his wife.

"Mayhap she don' want to share her business with you, Maybelle."

Maybelle snorted. "She's a woman needing help, aren't you dear?"

"I'm fine," she said, although she smiled gratefully at the woman, appreciating her concern. "I am simply tired, and I think I might take myself to bed."

"Ah, the exhaustion is beginning, is it not?" the woman asked knowingly, raising an eyebrow. Maria wasn't quite sure how to respond. The truth was, her mind was whirling with thoughts. With child? She knew that it was only a possibility and could not yet be the cause of her sickness, but as Hudson had said, there was a chance. How could she run away when she might have his child in her belly? It would go against everything he had ever wanted for his life, and she didn't even know how she was going to care for herself, let alone a baby.

"You best try to eat something," the woman said kindly. "An empty stomach will only be worse later on."

Maria nodded woodenly, having no desire to explain the situation, and picked up the spoon beside the plate, pushing around the food as she tried not to gag again. She didn't think she would be able to stomach the meat, but she managed a few potatoes and peas.

When she thought her eyes were likely to close as she sat in the chair, she paid for her meal and climbed the stairs, keeping her hood up and looking from one side to the next as she went. She was on the run, acting like a fugitive.

Which, she supposed, in a way she was.

She reached her room, eyeing it critically but telling herself it was a bed, so would have to do. Whether or not it was clean, she had no idea, so she took off her cloak and laid it over the mattress and blanket before taking the small wooden chair from the side of the room and wedging it under the door to try to prevent anyone from entering. She kept the ring and the broach — which she had thought to pawn whenever she reached her next destination as it would appear far too suspicious in London — and tucked them underneath the pillow.

Whether she would use them or not — or if she should return to Hudson with the possibility she was carrying his baby — she had no idea.

Then she fell to sleep fitfully, uncertainty preventing her from a truly deep sleep.

* * *

"I HEAR you've lost Lady Maria."

Hudson eyed his half-brother with a look as the duke stepped through Archibald's front door. Here he thought they were finding a common ground once more.

"He's joking," Juliana said, walking over to her brother to swat him on the arm before continuing into their small cooking area, where she began to prepare drinks for the lot of them. Behind the duke came his wife as well as his other sister, Lady Prudence, although this time Lady Winchester was not among them.

Instead, bringing up the rear was Archibald.

Juliana's menagerie of animals greeted them all with enthusiasm, the large, shaggy dog she called Max jumping all over Archibald in his joy to see him once more.

"We are here to formulate a plan," Archibald said as they all gathered around the room as they had previously. "Let's fight with each other and not against one another, all right?"

He eyed them all with a look, and even Giles nodded in agreement. Hudson wondered if this is why Archibald had been so successful building a business with a team of men.

"Now, I have my men out asking questions to determine if anyone knows where Maria might have gone. They're checking ports, stagecoaches, and inns to see if there is any description of her. In the meantime, I think we best find Dennison. Perhaps Remington and I should follow up there. As a duke, he can access places that I cannot."

"Very well," Hudson said. "And what should I do?"

"It's late. Go home. Get some rest."

"I hardly think that will be possible," Hudson said with a scoff. "I'll help your men look."

"They can do fine on their own."

"Let him help, Matthew," Juliana said softly, as her other dog, the small, mangy one named Lucy, came over and ate a sandwich off of Hudson's lap. He didn't care — he didn't have an appetite anyway. "Think if you were in his position. You'd have to *do* something. Besides, he knows her better than any of us do. He might get an inkling of where she has gone, could follow where others wouldn't be able to."

"Very well," Matthew said after a moment of consideration. "It's ten o'clock now. At one o'clock let's all meet back here. Then we can get some sleep and reconvene in the morning."

Hudson didn't agree, for he knew that there was no way he would sleep until he found Maria. She could try to protect him all she wanted, but nothing could ever break him more than losing her, in whatever manner that happened to be.

"Where will you go first?" Juliana asked him and he let out a breath, running a hand through his hair as he tried to determine just where she would have gone.

"Your grandmother told her to go to America."

"America?" Juliana asked, her eyes widening, pausing to kiss her husband on the cheek as he left, though not before he told her that she wasn't to leave the house, and that one of his men, a Mr. Green, would remain to ensure all was well and no one could enter who wasn't welcome. "My grandmother?"

"Yes. Apparently they had a conversation one day when your grandmother happened upon her while she was waiting for me."

"Interesting," Juliana mused. "My grandmother is certainly never one to keep her opinions to herself."

"No," Hudson said with a slight chuckle despite all they were up against. "She certainly does not."

"Would Maria have listened to her?"

"I know she didn't want to leave at all, until the fire convinced her," Hudson said. "But she had no money besides the slight bit I had paid her for her time working with me, and even that was minimal for she refused to accept much while living with me."

"That sounds like Maria."

Hudson nodded as he heard the flapping of wings overhead. "Please tell me that bird doesn't belong to you."

"Maggie? Why yes, actually, she does. At least, she decided she does."

"Will it shite on me?"

"She shouldn't."

"That is hardly reassuring."

"Well, if she does, she shall bring you a pretty trinket to make up for it."

Hudson eyed her in disbelief. "Your husband agrees with keeping it?"

"He doesn't have much choice," she said with a slight laugh before her expression turned contemplative. "I don't suppose…"

"What is it?"

"If you were Maria and had no money, no way to pay for passage anywhere, who would you turn to?"

Hudson frowned. "Someone who I knew would support my decision."

"Which she knew would not include any of us. Except—"

"Your grandmother." Hudson's head snapped up to look at her. "Do you think she would actually have helped her, without telling any of us?"

"If my grandmother believed that was the right decision

for Maria to make, then she most certainly would have supported her."

"I have to go."

"Very well," Juliana said with a nod. "Good luck. And do try to avoid my mother. Find Prudence, if you can."

Hudson nodded and slipped out the door, closing it behind him before Juliana's collection of animals could follow him out.

CHAPTER 21

*H*udson stared up at the grand expanse of the duke's manor. It was one thing to be invited to the home, but quite another to simply show up on the doorstep and expect to be welcomed — especially at this hour of night, although he knew many of the noble set would be accustomed to socializing at this time.

He was fortunate, however, when the door opened before he could even knock — revealing Lady Prudence herself, dressed in nightclothes.

"Dr. Lewis?" she said, raising her eyebrows. "What are you doing here?"

"It's a long story," he said, lifting his cap and raking a hand through his hair. "But I'm here to see your grandmother."

"I am sure she will welcome a handsome gentleman caller at this hour of night," she said with a slight curve of her lips, laughing when she saw Hudson's expression. "I am jesting. I shall see if I can find her. Come, we will deposit you in the small parlor that Juliana preferred before my mother hears word that you are here at this hour."

She looked around the corner, apparently ensuring the way was clear before she waved Hudson forward.

"How did you know I was here?" he murmured.

"My window faces the front of the house and I saw you lurking."

His spine stiffened slightly. "I would hardly call it lurking. I—"

"Just be glad it was me who saw you."

Soon enough he found himself in a rather feminine though comfortable sitting room with two writing desks and a small sofa. He waited rather impatiently until Lady Winchester arrived, still dressed in her evening wear.

"Dr. Lewis," she said, no surprise evident on her face. "I appreciate the call, although I must admit I am not as young as I used to be."

He rose and bowed to her, a slight smile on his lips despite the situation. "Your granddaughter seems to share your sense of humor, my lady."

"She is an intelligent one," she said, nodding to Prudence, who stepped through the door behind her and closed the door at her back. "Now, my daughter has, fortunately, gone to bed for the night but if Jameson or one of her other loyal servants sees you, then we will have some explaining to do. Not that it would bother me, but it is rather annoying to have to justify my every movement. What can I do for you?"

"I think you know why I'm here," he said, leaning forward with his elbows on the tops of his thighs.

"Do I?" she said, lifting a brow regally.

"Lady Maria."

"A lovely young woman."

"Grandmother," Prudence said from the door with a sigh. "Do you know something? Have you done something? Lady Maria is missing and there are men — including Giles — searching London for her as we speak."

"I told her that she should have spoken to you," Lady Winchester said, tapping her cane on the ground, and a slight rush of relief overcame Hudson at the assurance that Maria had left of her own accord and had not been forced.

"Where did she go?" he asked as gently as he could, trying not to rush the woman.

"That, I cannot tell you, for I do not know," she said, and the relief soon fell away. "All I know is that she became aware that staying was far too dangerous, for herself and for you, although you were the only one she truly cared about. After the fire she determined, as I had originally suggested, that it would be best she leave the city, away from anyone Dennison might have watching her. I suggested that she should have asked if you would accompany her, but she said she refused to force you to make that choice."

Hudson's hands clasped into fists. He knew Maria did what she had thought was right, but why would she take that choice away from him? It was his to make. For he would choose her, over and over again. His life was not the same without her in it.

"Did you give her money?" he asked, keeping his voice calm, even.

Lady Winchester nodded. "I gave her what I could — enough for her to hire a hack to convey her out of the city or to a port or stagecoach, I suppose. I also gave her a broach that she could pawn. I only hope she will receive the true value for it."

"What does the broach look like?" he asked, and she described it.

"Thank you," he said, rising to go.

"Dr. Lewis?" Lady Winchester called, and he turned to her.

"Yes?"

"That girl loves you with all of her heart. If you cannot

give her what she needs — to accompany her away from this city and that man who is after her — then let her go. For if she were to stay, it would only mean certain tragedy for both of you. I hate that Dennison would wield the power he does, but that is the way of it, and I cannot see the two of you able to win out against him."

Hudson nodded curtly. "I understand. Thank you, Lady Winchester."

He would have liked to have told her that she never should have sent Maria on her way without informing one of them — at least the duke — but he knew it was not his place to do so, that he would only insult her if he challenged her.

And so, he set out, trying to decide if he was Maria, just where he would go.

* * *

MARIA COULDN'T QUITE REMEMBER a night ever feeling longer than this one had.

Between trying to determine her own fate, worrying about how Hudson was feeling about her leaving him, and staring at the door, wondering if Lord Dennison was going to break in at any moment to steal her back, she hadn't slept overly well.

Then there was, of course, the words of the woman from the tavern swimming around in her mind.

What would she do if she was actually carrying Hudson's baby? She wouldn't know for some time, yet she couldn't rid the idea from her mind.

She sank down on the edge of the bed. What a fool she was, to run from one place to another, uncertain of what she was doing or where she was going or whether or not she had a child growing within her.

After all of this she wondered if Hudson would even want her anymore, or if he would consider her too flighty to handle for the rest of his life — especially considering she could not give him a family in the way he had always wanted.

Finally, she stood, splashed cold water on her face, cleaned her mouth out, and gripped the edges of the basin as she formulated a plan. She would leave London to escape the clutches of Lord Dennison — but she wouldn't go too far. When she arrived at her eventual destination, she would write to Hudson and explain everything. By then she would know for certain if there was a baby on his or her way, and he could decide what he wanted to do without feeling any obligation toward her.

Yes, she decided.

She would make her own way.

Maria wrapped her cloak around her shoulders, then strode over to the door and moved the chair. She unlocked the door, twisted the knob open — and came face to face with her future, whether she liked it or not.

* * *

"Oh, thank God."

He reached through the door, pulling her into his arms, clutching her tightly against him. She stiffened for long enough that he lost his breath, wondering if she was as happy to see him as he was she, before she returned his embrace, wrapping her arms around his neck and holding him just as close.

She was here. She was safe. He had reached her before Dennison had. And he was not letting her go.

"How did you find me?"

"That's a long story," Hudson said, allowing his heart rate

to finally return to normal as he only now realized the amount of panic he had been moving through after the entire ordeal of the night. "But first, we should go find everyone who has been waiting to hear news of where you are."

"Everyone?"

"Yes," he said, pulling back away from her to look into her eyes. They were as blue as ever, except now they were red-rimmed and puffy, and he wondered if she had slept a wink.

"Are you all right? Are you hurt? Do you need to sleep?"

She shook her head at all of his questions, although her gaze flew to the ground.

"Hudson," she managed, squeezing his hands, "I am so sorry. I never meant for any of this to happen, nor to scare anyone. But I cannot... I cannot go with you."

He felt as though he had been punched in the gut, but he remained as calm as he could, not wanting to scare her or push her even further away from him.

"Why not?"

"Because I would only put you in danger once more!" she cried out, her hands flying into the air. She took one of his hands in hers and pulled him back into the room, likely so they could have more privacy than they would standing out in the middle of the balcony overlooking the courtyard below. "The reasons for me leaving have not changed. If I remain with you in London, you will not be safe from Lord Dennison. He knows that I am with you, and he will continue to come after you, until he achieves his aim. I cannot allow that to happen."

She reached a shaky hand beneath her cloak and retrieved the note from her pocket.

"After the fire... I was given this."

Hudson took the note from her, his brow furrowing and his lips clenching together as he read it.

"Why did you not tell me about this?"

"Because you would have told me that we would handle it — that you would keep me safe. But it was time for me to do something that would keep *you* safe. And I couldn't do that by remaining with you."

"If you felt so strongly about leaving, I would have gone with you."

"I couldn't ask you to do that," she said, sniffing now, and he felt a boor for causing her any unhappiness, but he wasn't sure how else to make her understand.

"Maria." He set his jaw, staring at her intensely. "If you do not want me, tell me now. Otherwise, we come together. Where you go, I go. Everything else is a want, but not a necessity. You, I need. I love you, Maria. I have committed my life to you, and nothing is ever going to change that — except you and your own decision. If you feel the same, then we will handle whatever comes. Together."

He could tell the moment he had finally gotten through to her, when she realized the truth of what he was saying, the choice he had made, despite what she had thought was in his best interests.

Tears began running down her cheeks, and he gathered her hands in his, wanting to bring her close again, but sensing she needed the time to say what she needed to.

"Hudson, I love you too. So much. And I want to be with you. I just cannot stand the thought of anything happening to you because of me. I didn't want to force you to make the choice between me and your life and I thought it would be best that I go."

"Maria." He leaned in and placed his forehead against hers. "You are my life."

She nodded as she began crying more earnestly now, and this time he gave in to the temptation and he pulled her close, resting her head on his chest as he rocked her in his arms.

"Where shall we go? Where should we live?"

"As it happens, I'm not sure that we will actually need to leave London."

"What?" She pulled back and away from him, looking up into his face. "Why do you say that?"

"It's been a long night for all of us," he said, his chin set grimly. "Archibald and his men have learned a few things… and they also have a plan. I cannot say that I approve of it — but I will let him explain and you can make your own decision."

"Very well…" she said, and he could tell she was curious but willing to wait before asking further questions.

"We will go to the duke's manor," he said. "It is closely safeguarded with the exterior wall, and I doubt that Dennison would try anything on the premises."

"What about the dowager duchess?"

Hudson couldn't help a slight chuckle at that. "Wouldn't you know it, but the duke has finally decided to stand up to her."

She laughed slightly through her tears. "I suppose he has done so already, with his own marriage and then allowing Juliana's."

"True, but this time he actually told her how it is going to be, which is something else entirely."

She nodded as they walked to the door together, and then she looked up at him, question in her eyes.

"Hudson, how did you find me?"

"It was in part due to considering where I thought you would be most likely to go, based on the conversation between you and Lady Winchester. It was also partially due to Archibald's men, who helped me ask after you in every port and inn we could find. And then there is the other factor you likely never considered."

"Which is?"

"We are drawn together, Maria. No matter what tries to separate us, there is one thing I can promise you — our hearts will always find their way back to one another."

CHAPTER 22

*M*aria felt like she was in some kind of dream as she allowed Hudson to lead her to his gig, which was waiting in the stables of the inn. She was somewhat apprehensive about returning to one of the locations where Dennison might find her, but if she was choosing to return, then she would have to trust Hudson and his instincts. If he said they had a plan, then she would have to believe they had a plan that would work, and she would do her part to ensure it came to fruition.

The hour was early, but this part of the city was already bustling with activity, as residents were well into their day of work. Maria stayed tucked into Hudson's side as he meandered the gig through the street, marvelling as they went through the differences between neighborhoods as one slowly merged into another.

The streets were congested and would have been slow moving, but Hudson drove with an ease that had come from years of navigating the streets with an emergency awaiting him. She supposed that this could count as one.

Finally, they arrived in front of the duke's mansion. It

often reminded Maria of a country estate tucked away in the middle of London, which she supposed, in a way, it was. It was one of the few such mansions in London that remained a private residence, and sometimes she forgot that it all could have been hers, had the duke chosen to marry her as had been expected.

But when she looked over at Hudson, she knew that she would live in the smallest of hovels if it meant being with him. And that, she decided, was what it truly meant to love someone.

The entire household was obviously in understanding of what was happening, as Jameson allowed them entrance and told them that the grooms would look after Hudson's horse and gig. He then led them into the drawing room, where Maria found the entire Remington family awaiting them.

"Maria, thank goodness," Juliana said, standing from her place on the sofa and running to her, wrapping her arms around her. Beside her sat her husband, and across from them on the matching sofa was the duke, who had one arm wrapped protectively around his rather pregnant wife. Prudence sat in a chair, a teacup in hand, while Lady Winchester perched regally beside her. Even the dowager duchess was there, sitting with her back straight in a chair against the wall.

"Lady Maria, how lovely to see you," she said as if Maria had come to visit for tea. "I am sure your mother will be ever so relieved to know you are well."

"Mother, we discussed this," Giles said impatiently. "We are not sharing the information about Lady Maria's whereabouts with anyone — including her mother."

"That does not mean that I cannot express how I feel."

"Very well," the duke said. "You feel relieved. Now, we should discuss what has occurred and what we are to do.

Archibald, why do you not tell everyone what we have discovered so far and what we expect will happen next."

The detective nodded, leaning forward as he cast his eyes around the room. "Remington and I spent most of our night tracking the earl. He didn't do much that we would not have expected. He began the night at a dinner party but quickly left after the polite hour for a club that was much less reputable. However, on the way there he made a stop at a tavern in Covent Garden to meet with a man who is known for his... less savory business practices. After Dennison continued on, we questioned the man and he finally admitted to following you, Lady Maria, although he refused to admit to anything else, including starting the fire."

Maria shivered at the thought of someone watching all of her movements.

"I believe that Lord Dennison himself started the fire," she said, obviously surprising all of them — including Hudson.

He leaned back and looked at her.

"Because of the note?"

"That, yes, but there was something else that I forgot to tell you about."

She reached into the pocket beneath her cloak and pulled out Dennison's ring.

"I found this on the floor of your house, at the door of the study. Perhaps it came off his hand as he threw in whatever was required to start the fire. It's his crest. I remember it from his coach."

Hudson's hand fisted and she knew that she likely wasn't helping his sentiments, but it was important to share all of the information she held.

Archibald took the ring from her, staring at it grimly.

"One of my men also spoke to Jane, the maid, to ensure all was well in her new position. She gave him the names of a few other maids who could also confirm what she had told us about Dennison and the maid she believes he killed. Of course, the word of a few maids will not result in any persecution."

Maria reached over to seek Hudson's hand for comfort.

"What do we do now?"

Mr. Archibald and the duke exchanged a glance before looking over to her and Hudson. "We believe we need to draw out the earl. If we can convince the magistrate to come with us and he hears the earl's admission of murder as well as his intent to pursue you, that, along with the backing of the duke, should be enough to convince the House of Lords to try him."

Hudson shook his head. "I do not think we should do it."

"Why not?" Juliana asked him, seeming genuinely curious.

"It puts Maria in danger. What if we don't succeed in our plan? Then he will have found her and we would have no recourse anymore to keep her safe from him. He would insist she return with him, and then she would be in more danger than she would ever have been."

Maria swallowed hard at the thought. She looked to the duke, the man who would know better than anyone else here what the chances of success would be.

"Do you believe it will work?"

He grimaced. "I'd say the chances are pretty equal either way. If we are unsuccessful, however, we would need a plan for you and Hudson to escape, and you could never come back to London — likely even to England."

Maria looked Hudson in the eyes, and he gave a slight shrug as if to say it was entirely her choice.

"Very well," she said with a resolute nod. "We should do it."

"Are you sure?" Hudson asked. "This plan would include using you to draw him to you. We would have to make him think that you were alone, likely at my mother's house. We would come shortly afterward, but there might be a few minutes when it would only be you in the room with him as we would need you to convince him to talk."

"I can do it," she said, even though inside, she was shaking slightly at the thought of facing the earl once again, especially on her own. But now she knew she was stronger than she had thought she was, and that she could do anything — especially knowing that she had Hudson and the entire Remington family at her side. "When do you hope to go ahead?"

"I think tomorrow is best," Archibald said. "We will plant the word of your whereabouts and then get this done as quickly as possible. Hopefully, then, Lady Maria, you can have your life back."

She looked at Hudson next to her. She needed to do this, not only for herself but for all of the other women that the earl had harmed or who he could harm in the future.

For she already had the life that she wanted, because she had Hudson, no matter what lay ahead of them.

The rest, they would figure out together.

* * *

HUDSON'S PROFESSION was one that depended on his utmost attention in every situation.

Which was why it was most difficult to continue to go about his business, knowing what was to come and the evening events that lay ahead of them with no surety of what the results might be.

But he could hardly turn away anyone who showed up at his mother's door looking for his help. He ensured that Maria accompanied him this time, as he was unable to let her out of his sight, even for a moment. She understood and went along willingly, and in fact was even more present than he was at each house call.

"How are you so calm?" he asked as they left the Bloomsburys. He had made sure that Maria stayed in the front room with Mrs. Bloomsbury this time, not trusting Mr. Bloomsbury to be anywhere near her, although the man did seem to be in a much better place today, as he shamefully apologized to Hudson for all that had occurred the time before.

"It is from a lifetime of learning to hide emotion and put on a face, no matter what I am feeling inside," she said. "I will admit to you that my stomach is a bundle of nerves about what is to come tonight."

"Are you still sure you want to do this?"

"I am," she said, and he noted the set of her jaw, the resolution in her eyes.

Hudson had known that she had to be the one to make this choice, but he understood, then, how important it was for her to go ahead with this. He may yearn to do all in his power to protect her, to keep her from harm, but if he told her what to do or prevented her from following through on her decision, then he would be no better than her reprobate of a husband.

"I need to do this, Hudson," she said fiercely. "I need to do this for the women he harmed. I need to do this for the women that he could harm in the future. And I need to do this for me. It is the only way that I can truly move on, that I can put the past behind me. Besides, in the meantime, we also might learn more about what he has done to the Remington family, or how he might threaten them in the future."

Hudson nodded as he pushed open the door to his mother's house. "I understand."

"Thank you," Maria said, bestowing a slightly watery

smile upon him before they continued in. "That means more to me than you know."

He began to lean in to kiss her, forgetting where they were, but was prevented from doing so when his mother appeared from the room beyond.

"There you are!" she exclaimed. "I've been worried about you. You took far too long."

"I am doing house calls, Mother," he said as patiently as he could. "You should know better than anyone how long they can take."

"Yes, but that was before you were in danger," she said, her eyes flitting to Maria. She was beginning to begrudgingly accept Maria, but she hadn't quite overcome Maria's noble birth or the fact Hudson had been in danger and had lost his home and aspects of his practice.

She did, however, soften towards her when she learned that Maria had also been wronged by the Duke of Warwick, despite Maria's protests that it had all worked out for the best.

"Mother, are you preparing to depart for Sir Willoughby's?"

"Yes," she said, pursing her lips together. She was also not completely enamored with the thought of her house being used in their plan to bait the earl, but it was the only logical place where the earl might believe without suspicion that Maria would be left alone. "He should be here any minute to collect me in his carriage and then you can continue with this scheme of yours."

She stepped close to Maria, her face softening as she tilted her head to look at her.

"I hope that all goes well and that you are able to be rid of that awful man."

Maria smiled tightly at her, and Hudson knew exactly what she was thinking. They had shared with his mother every aspect of the plan except one — the part in which they would have to leave if everything went awry. He wasn't sure his mother would be able to handle the thought of his departure, but now he didn't know how to say goodbye to her.

He finally allowed himself to lean in and embrace her.

"Thank you, Mother," he said in her ear. "For everything."

"Of course," she said, blinking in surprise at his show of affection. "I shall see you later this evening."

There was a rumble outside the window as Sir Willoughby arrived with his carriage, which meant it was time for the next part of the evening to commence.

CHAPTER 23

*M*aria stood outside of Mrs. Lewis' house, trying not to look nervous, but rather attempt to make it appear that this was just another day.

Juliana arrived shortly as planned, making her exuberance obvious as she rushed down the street.

"Maria!" she called out. "I just heard the news!"

Maria and Hudson had decided that there would be one sure way to draw out the earl. He would be enraged if he thought another man's babe was in his wife's belly.

It was also a risk, of course, for if he captured Maria and she was with child, the baby would be his as well, no matter the true father.

Archibald had confirmed that there was still a man following Maria, and they had ensured he was watching when Juliana ran to the doorstep.

"Is it unbelievable, is it not?" Maria called out, not nearly as adept as Juliana at acting out this scene but giving her best effort. "I am to be a mother!"

That caused a few heads to turn, but no one who they knew particularly well.

Juliana rushed over and embraced Maria, squeezing her a little tighter in silent support before she leaned back. "I must hear everything!" she said. "Do you have time now?"

"I do," she said with a nod. "Come in, as Hudson must leave soon for an engagement."

"Are you to be alone all night?"

"I am, as his mother is also out."

"I'm so sorry I cannot stay, but we shall have a few minutes to catch up," Juliana said, before they went into the building.

There, Hudson and Archibald were waiting.

"Was that loud enough?" Juliana asked.

"Jules, I think people two streets over likely heard you," Archibald said, although there was a smile on his face.

"Good," she said. "Then hopefully the message returns to Lord Dennison that Maria will be alone."

"Have you spoken with the magistrate?" she asked Archibald, who confirmed with a nod.

"He is not keen on this plan, particularly as Dennison is a peer of high ranking and he could not actually arrest him, of course, but because Remington insisted that he would be a reputable witness, he will be here. The two of them will be in the back room."

"And the two of you?" Maria asked, hoping they would be close to help should anything go wrong."

"We will be outside, ready to come in after his confession is complete. We will wait and listen at the front window. Then he will be trapped from the back and the front so he will not be able to escape."

"Very well," she said. "And if… if we are unable to extract a confession and he tries to make me return with him?"

Hudson's face hardened, but it was Mr. Archibald who answered.

"Remington will send his carriage, the one without the

crest so it will be unremarkable. It will go around the back and will wait near the stable down the road. You will have to make a run for it and then it will then convey you out of London."

"Let's hope that doesn't happen," Maria said nervously, and Hudson walked over and stilled her hands with his.

"But if it does, then so be it," he said. "We will come out of this, one way or another."

She nodded and took a breath. A few more minutes and Juliana would leave, followed by Hudson, before Archibald would exchange places with Remington and the magistrate through the back door.

Then it would be all up to Maria.

She only hoped she could handle this.

SHE OPENED the door and made a show of kissing Hudson on the cheek before he left.

"I do wish I could accompany you," she said, loudly enough for any onlookers to hear. "Have a fine time. I shall be here waiting!"

"Be sure to lock the door," he said, and then couldn't help himself from drawing her in and giving her another kiss. "I love you."

"I love you too," she said, their words holding much more meaning than if this was a simple departure.

"Be safe," he said softly.

"You too."

Then with that he was off without a glance behind him, although Maria could feel that pull he had spoken of, even as he walked away from her.

She stepped back inside, emptiness surrounding her,

before the back door opened and she whirled around, only to see that it was the duke and a man she didn't recognize, who must be the magistrate. She nodded to them as they continued onto one of the back bedrooms, the one that Maria had been using since they had arrived here.

Then she sat on the sofa and waited.

As it happened, she didn't have to wait long. She had been expecting him to come later in the evening, after darkness had fallen, but it seemed the trap they had set had been too tempting, for there was a knock on the door not a half hour later.

"Who is it?" Maria said as the banging continued. She stood on the other side, hearing his loud breathing, his voice as it called out to her with no attempt to hide his identity.

"I know you are in there, Maria. Open the damn door!"

She didn't respond, for she knew that he wouldn't expect her to, although she did begin to slowly back away, not wanting to take the full brunt of his anger if and when he did manage to open it.

Then suddenly, the door crashed open with a bang, and her husband was standing there at the threshold. His eyes were slightly wild, his nostrils flaring, his usually well-kept hair standing on end as he stared her down.

"Did you truly think you could outrun me forever?" he asked. "What did you believe? That you could leave your husband and start a new life for yourself, here with that bastard while you carry another in your belly? The joke is on you, for like it or not, that will be my heir you carry in there. Come. I am taking you back and will show you how a wife of mine is supposed to behave."

Maria straightened her spine as she backed up through the room, closer to the bedroom so that the duke and the magistrate would be able to better hear the conversation.

"I will not go with you."

He sneered. "Do you honestly think you have a choice? You are my *wife*. You do as I tell you to do."

"I refuse to live with a murderer," she said, spitting the words out, and he threw his head back and laughed at her.

"Who told you that? Let me guess, one of the maids? Women who belong to me, just as you do."

"They do not," she said fiercely. "They work for you. They are not enslaved to you."

"No," he grinned wickedly. "But you are."

"Would you do to me what you did to that girl?" she asked, backing up farther as he advanced toward her now, scaring her with the predatory smile on his face.

"I just had a little fun with her," he said, shrugging. "It went too far. She wasn't strong enough for it. You, however, I think I could handle. You're built for this life."

"A little fun," she said, trying to keep her voice from shaking while goading him to tell her more. "What kind of fun?"

"Are your delicate ears ready to hear it?" he said, raising a brow. "Or are you looking forward to it now that the doctor has sampled you?"

The thought of this man ever touching her caused her to recoil in revulsion, but she didn't say anything, hoping that he would want to continue to hear himself talk.

"Sometimes a woman enjoys having the air taken from her as I take my pleasure," he said, his eyes shining as he said it. "I just forgot to give it back to her!"

He laughed then, manically almost, and Maria swallowed hard.

"Then she died?"

"I suppose," he said with a shrug. "I did not stay long to see if she began breathing again. My valet took care of it."

Maria gagged as she nearly threw up once more, only this time she didn't know if it was from her nausea or revulsion or a combination of both.

"I heard you were going to kill me," she said now, hoping he would admit further crimes, but he simply studied her, his eyes beginning at her head and following her body down to her toes, causing her to shiver.

"I actually haven't decided yet," he said. "Now that I know you are fertile, perhaps you will do after all. Maybe I'll have to test you, see what you can withstand."

He snaked his arm out toward her, and she tried to continue to back away, but she had run into the wall. She knew she could cry out and the duke would come running from the bedroom beyond, but first she wanted to try to force him to admit that he had pursued the Remington family.

"What about the duke?" she asked desperately as he gripped her arm, his hand tightening painfully.

"What duke?" he practically spat in her face, and she realized that he had lost most reason now.

"The Duke of Warwick," she said. "Why are you after their family?"

"Why do you care about him?" he asked, his eyes boring into her. "He didn't want you, in case you do not recall. I can now see why."

"Let me go," she said, trying to shake his arm loose, but he only gripped her tighter, his other arm coming around her.

"Don't you understand?" he sneered. "You have no power over me. You are mine to do with as I wish. Perhaps you need to learn that the hard way, before we leave. Or maybe I'll wait for the doctor and make him watch before I kill you."

She gasped as he turned her around, and she struggled, trying to extricate herself from his grip, but it was no use. He was too strong. She cried out, and within seconds, both the bedroom door and the front door burst open, revealing four men — the magistrate with shock on his face, while the other three appearing ready to commit murder themselves.

The earl whirled Maria around, holding her back against his body, and as she tried to free herself, Hudson rushed forward until he stopped, frozen on the spot.

When something cold and sharp brushed against Maria's throat, she instantly realized why.

"Do not come any closer," the earl said, his voice right in her ear. "Or I will slit her throat. I care not who is watching. She is my wife, and I can do as I please."

"Except kill her," the magistrate said, his voice slightly uneasy. "You cannot kill her."

"Can I not?" he said, and Maria tried not to let any sound that would reveal her panic escape.

"No, you cannot."

"Have you murdered before, then?" the duke asked, taking just one step forward, his usual rather jovial face hard and unrelenting. "My father, perhaps?"

The earl snorted. "Your father was an ass, and I am glad that he is dead. Believe me, most people are. But I did not kill him."

"You wanted to, though, didn't you?"

The earl shrugged, the knife scraping against Maria's throat as he did so.

"He's better off dead, that is for certain. I would never have done so, however. I am not stupid enough to kill a duke."

"No, just a maid," Hudson said, the anger firm in his voice, and Maria wished with everything within her that she could launch herself into his arms.

"I did not kill the duke," Dennison repeated and despite

how much she hated him, Maria was inclined to believe him. "But I can tell you who did."

"Can you now?" The duke raised a brow.

"Lord Trundelle," he said smugly. "The man despised the duke, spoke a few times about how much better off we would be if he were dead. His entire fortune was tied up with him, although I don't suppose you've cashed in on that debt yet, have you Warwick? Need to find those vowels?"

"Why are you telling me this?" the duke asked, eyeing him. "I thought the two of you were in this together."

"We had a similar interest, let's put it that way," Dennison said. "But I've found my way out of this."

"How?"

"Nothing you need to worry about just now. Trundelle is the one to watch. Look into him, and you will find your killer."

"But why come after my family now?" the duke pressed, and Maria finally saw what he was doing. He was keeping Dennison's attention while Hudson slowly began to circle around the room so that he would be closer to her and the earl.

"Why are you asking me?" the earl said. "That's a question for the man himself. As for me? I am just going to take my wife and go now. We have… *plans* for this evening."

He began to walk Maria to the door, and she took the steps with him — for she had seen what he didn't. As they began to move, Hudson launched himself from the corner of the room, a flash of something that she couldn't quite see in his hand, and then they all went down in a pile. She covered her arms over her head in protection, and then Hudson was there too, leaning over her, keeping her safe in the cocoon of his arms.

She closed her eyes as shouts ricocheted around the room, and when she finally opened them at Hudson's soothing voice in her ear, she stopped breathing for a moment.

For on the floor was her husband, his eyes and mouth open, but there was no air escaping his mouth, no rise of his chest.

He was dead.

CHAPTER 24

*H*udson turned Maria around and cradled her head so that her face was in his chest to prevent her from the gore before her, but it was too late — he had known it as soon as he heard her shriek.

He looked up, his gaze meeting first Archibald's and then his half-brother's as they all stared at one another in horrified understanding.

For it could be said that Hudson killed the earl, even if that had not been his intent.

The magistrate displayed no sign of emotion as he walked over to the body, taking in first the syringe that was sticking out of the earl's arm and then the knife that was wedged into his chest.

"He's definitely dead," he said grimly. "The knife luckily — or unluckily in his case — found a space between his ribs and punctured his heart or lung. I'm not certain which."

"I only meant to remove him from Maria," Hudson said, the emotions nearly overwhelming him at the moment. For as fearful as he was that he might be hanged for the killing of an earl, at least now he knew with all certainty that Maria was free. No matter what happened, she would not be subjected to that monster. Even if he was not here to see it, she would have a life.

But damn, he hoped that he would be able to share that life with her.

"The syringe you wielded struck his arm," the magistrate said, removing his cap and scratching his head. "And the knife was in his own hand. So as far as I can tell… he did this to himself."

Hudson looked up, a slight bit of hope filling his chest.

"I'm a physician," he said, hoping that the man would be reasonable, would understand his words. "I would never kill a man. I do all I can for even the worst of them."

"I understand," said the magistrate, looking up to judge the duke's reaction. Remington was staring at him with that ducal air of his that he was beginning to adopt likely without even realizing it, as he adjusted to his new role. "Had I not been here for the entirety of this evening, I might have more questions. But I believe I have seen and heard enough. I shall make an official report that this was an accident, that he died by his own hand while threatening the rest of you. As for the maid's death, well, it is not likely that much will be done, but—"

"But at least there is some justice," Hudson heard Maria say quietly, and he wrapped an arm around her shoulders and squeezed her gently.

She was right. And he hoped that she would understand that she had been brave, that she had done more than most people would have been able to do under the circumstances.

And the second he was able to, he was going to have her in front of that altar.

"He never admitted to burning down your home," she said forlornly, looking up at Hudson now. He shrugged.

"It's all right. We have his ring at the scene and the fire

brigade already determined that it was set deliberately. I will have the insurance, and we can rebuild."

She nodded slowly and then looked up at him.

"I have a few ideas, actually," she said somewhat shyly, and he smiled down at her.

"I would be happy to hear them."

He looked up at the magistrate now. "What more do you need from us? If we can clean this up before my mother returns, that would be much appreciated."

"Oh, my goodness," Maria said, her hand covering her mouth. "There is a dead man in your mother's home." She looked up at him wide-eyed. "Whatever will she say?"

"She'll likely be angrier about Remington being in her home than the dead earl," he said, only half jesting as the duke snorted.

"Why don't we allow the magistrate to take care of this while we update the rest of the family?" he asked, looking at Hudson, who nodded slowly, sensing that, perhaps, this was the start of something new with his brother — and the family he had never known he had, nor never known he wanted. "If we wait any longer, I'm sure Juliana and Prudence will appear on the doorstep themselves."

"I wouldn't put it past them," Maria said, trying to jest, but Hudson followed her eyes down to her hands, both noticing that they were shaking. He gently placed an arm around her back and turned her, leading her out the door while motioning to the duke to follow.

"I'll go prepare the gig if you will stay with her, Remington?" he asked, taking a chance on the man — his brother.

"Very well," Remington said with a nod, seemingly understanding the importance of Hudson's request. Before Hudson left for the stable, he motioned to the side for Remington to follow him a few steps away from Maria, who was staring down the street.

"She is shocked from the entire evening, which is understandable," he said in a low voice in the duke's ear. "I believe she should be fine but let us get her out of here and return to your house as quickly as we can, if you do not mind."

"Agreed," Remington said. "The magistrate should be able to take care of everything else."

Soon enough they were sitting once more in the duke's opulent drawing room. Hudson would have preferred that Maria rest on her own, but she had insisted she wanted to sit with the entirety of the family to update them on all that had occurred.

Hudson sat on one side of her, Juliana on the other, providing her support as Remington told the tale as succinctly as possible.

Juliana and Prudence, for once, as far as Hudson was aware, listened attentively, without interrupting, except for the odd gasp of surprise.

When Remington finished the story, Juliana turned to Maria and placed her hand on hers.

"You were very brave."

"She was," Hudson said.

Juliana turned to him. "And there was no talk of you being blamed for this?"

"Not by the magistrate," Hudson said. "I would be slightly concerned about the House of Lords becoming involved, but with Remington's influence there, hopefully that shouldn't be much threat."

Juliana fixed Giles with a stare. "You would never let that happen, would you Giles?"

"Of course not," he said, before clearing his throat slightly. "Although I have not been part of the House long, I will do all I can to keep Lewis' name clear. I know this is a rather... unconventional situation we find ourselves in as a family, Lewis, but I'd like to ask for your forgiveness again — and to tell you that the doors here are always open to you. We would appreciate having you part of our lives, more than you would know."

Hudson met the duke's eyes, so like his own, and hesitated for just a moment before he nodded slowly. The dowager duchess, who until now had sat quietly, snorted slightly, but her mother hit her in the shins with her cane before she could say anything else. Hudson was aware that he might never win her over, but he could certainly understand why she might take issue with his presence.

"Thank you," he said quietly. "I appreciate it. And Your Grace," he said, addressing the duke's mother now, "I understand that it likely isn't easy to have me in your life, I do. My mother never had any intentions of coming between you and your husband — in fact, I cannot imagine a person who despised him more than any other in this world."

She raised her eyes in surprise at that, and too late, Hudson realized just what he had said and the implications it might portray in regard to the duke's murder — implications that he would like removed as far from his mother as possible.

"That being said, she holds nothing against the rest of the family," he added as quickly as he could without being obvious that he was trying to recover from his previous words. These ones weren't exactly truthful as his mother had been more than clear that she wanted nothing to do with any of the Remingtons, but she would never do anything to hurt any of them — of that, he was sure.

"I see," the dowager duchess said, although she eyed him critically, and he had a feeling that she might have more to say about it to the duke.

"Giles," Prudence said, leaning forward now, "when Dennison said that we should look into Trundelle, do you suppose he was telling the truth, or do you think he was trying to avert suspicion from himself?"

The duke sighed as he lifted his hands. "It's hard to know for certain. I suppose we will have to speak more to Archibald about it once he finishes with… everything… tonight. We'll have to see where Trundelle was when Juliana was taken, although the chances are high that someone hired him."

"Do you think whoever it was has given up?" the dowager duchess asked hopefully. "Nothing has happened since Juliana was abducted."

"No," Giles said, and Hudson knew then that he likely hadn't shared with his mother that someone had tried a second time to take Juliana, shortly before she and Archibald had married. "However, that doesn't mean that it has stopped. I do not want to continue to live my life unable to take a drink unless I see it actually poured from a decanter, or ensure that I do not walk around a corner without taking a wide turn so I can see what is waiting for me. I've about had quite enough of this, and I am sure the rest of you have too. We drew out the earl tonight. Perhaps we can work out a plan for something similar with whoever is coming after us."

His wife looked up at him, worry on her face. "Are you certain that is a good idea?"

He immediately leaned over her, his concern evident. Hudson knew he was protective of the new duchess to begin with, but even more so now that she was expecting. Which reminded him that Maria could be in the same condition, and he reached over and squeezed her hand once more. As much as he wanted to help the Remington family and do what he could to ensure their safety, he also wanted Maria to be able to rest and recover from all that had happened to her — and he was eager for time alone, just the two of them.

"It might not be the best of ideas, but it's a necessary one,"

Remington said, his jaw set firmly. "Bringing a child into this world is worrying enough without the addition of someone threatening our family. Now that Maria is here and safe from Dennison, we will focus on what is to come next."

"What are you going to do now?" Lady Winchester was the one posing the question to Maria, and while Hudson respected the woman, he still couldn't help his slight annoyance that she had helped Maria leave him without a word to him. "You are still Lady Dennison — without the monster anymore."

Maria nodded her head slowly. "I am — for now."

She looked over at Hudson with a slight smile and he nodded. He had much to say to her regarding that, although he would prefer to wait until the two of them were alone.

"I do not think I can return to his home, however — to any of them. His family was not exactly welcoming to begin with."

"Lady Christina," Juliana said with a shiver, as she always did when she mentioned the earl's sister, "would be a nightmare to live with. I cannot stand to be in her presence for a minute let alone an entire meal."

Maria nodded.

"I suppose I should go back to my parents' residence. They no longer will feel obligated to return me to anyone. Then... well, we shall see what comes next."

She met Hudson's eyes once more, and he was suddenly done with this meeting and the family — for now. He appreciated all of their support, but he needed a moment with Maria — and he needed it now.

"As Maria's physician, I would highly advise that she should rest now," he said, clearing his throat, ignoring Juliana's smirk and the knowing gazes from around the room. "We best be going."

"Why do you not stay the night?" the duchess asked. "It is

rather late, and you will not want to return so late. We have plenty of space."

She looked to her husband. "Do you not agree, Giles?"

"Of course," he said. "I shall speak to Jameson. We can also send word to your mother."

"Very well," Hudson said, knowing but not willing to consider whether or not his mother might stay the night at Sir Willoughby's. "Thank you — to all of you. I do appreciate all you have done for me."

"You are family," Juliana said with a small shrug, and he couldn't help the warm glow in his chest at her words.

Which only increased as he and Maria were led out of the drawing room and to their respective bedrooms.

CHAPTER 25

*M*aria didn't have to wait long before the knock sounded on her bedroom door.

She opened it without even looking, knowing who it would be. Emma had already sent her lady's maid to assist Maria, even though she tried to tell her that she didn't need one anymore, not now that she had become so accustomed to fending for herself — although she'd had Hudson to help her. But Emma insisted, and so Maria took the small luxury, for tonight at least.

"I was wondering how long it would take you to appear," she said with a small laugh, and Hudson raised an eyebrow at her.

"I could hardly arrive at the same time as the maid," he said.

"Are you afraid to cause a scandal?" she asked, and he chuckled.

"We are far past that."

He stepped through the door toward her and slipped his arms around her waist. She responded by drawing close to him, placing her head against his chest.

"Are you all right?" he asked. "Truly?"

"Yes," she said, nodding her head into him. "I cannot say that I ever imagined something like this would happen to me, but here we are. It is actually much better than what could have been."

"It is."

"What about you?" she asked, leaning back and looking up into his eyes. "I'm sure you had never expected to be the one inflicting damage upon a person."

"No," he said, shaking his head as he lifted a hand and ran his finger down the side of her face, "but I am also aware that Dennison did this to himself — that I was only trying to save you and had no intention of doing him irreparable injury. You are unharmed, and that is all that matters."

"I am more than unharmed. And Hudson?"

"Yes?"

"I am no longer married."

"You are not," he said, and she looked up at him, wondering if there was a reason he had not yet suggested they wed. "Would you mind being married again so quickly after the last time? I know society will expect you to mourn but if you do happen to be with child, we should do all we can to protect the babe's parentage. There will be suspicions enough as it is."

She smiled. It was as she had suspected... and hoped — that he hadn't wanted to push her into anything too quickly despite his own intentions.

"Since I do not consider my first marriage to have been a true one, I would rather like that," she said.

"Good," he said with a wide grin. "You will be my wife, then? The wife of a physician is not necessarily an easy one."

She laughed. "Oh, Hudson, I think we are far beyond considering what kind of lifestyle we will live," she said. "We were willing to run away to America and start anew. I believe living as the wife of a gentleman is far from a difficulty."

"Very good," he said, relief evident on his face. "Then, if that is a yes, how soon would you like to marry?"

"That most certainly is a yes, and as soon as possible," she said, and he finally leaned down and took her face in his hands, kissing her soundly.

"I love you, you know."

"I most certainly do," she responded. "Would you like to show me how much?"

"Here?" he asked, looking around them, and then at the door.

"We both have a tendency to follow the rules, do we not?" she asked with a grin.

"We do."

She leaned in, her mouth just beside his ear, and whispered, "I think it's time we break them."

"Goodness," he said, his lips curling into a sly grin of his own. "Just what am I to do with a woman like you?"

"Should I be nervous?" she asked, teasing, but when his smile dropped, she realized that he would always be understanding, would recognize just what she had faced and would do all he could to ensure that she never felt that fear again.

He looked her in the eye before his forehead came to hers.

"Never," he vowed fiercely. "I will only protect you."

His lips came down on hers, at first softly, but then hungrily as he tasted, teased, drank her in.

They had promised one another a lifetime together, yes — that had never changed — but now they knew that nothing would stand between them, nothing would keep them apart, and they could build the life they wanted without fear of anyone threatening to tear it all apart or rip Maria away from him.

He ran his hands through her hair, already let down for

bed, wrapping her curls around his fingers. He wondered if their child would have hair that coiled like hers, or the same straight, dark hair that he had inherited from the duke — a man he never knew, nor would he have wanted to — but who he could now acknowledge as his father.

Maria backed up until they were next to the bed, but before he laid her down, he slipped her wrapper off her shoulders, trailing his hands along the soft skin that was bared to him before he lifted her nightgown over her head. He made quick work of his own clothing until they were skin to skin, then lifted her gently in his arms before placing her on the bed beneath him.

"I am not so fragile, you know," she said, a smile on her lips, and he nodded.

"I know. I just want you to know how special you are to me. I promise to always take care of you."

She placed her finger on his nose. "I know that. I do. And you need to know that I will take care of you in turn — that is a promise."

He nodded his understanding as his lips took hers again, harder this time as if to show her that he understood she was not the fragile woman all had considered her to be, but a woman of strength.

And after he stroked her long enough to ensure that she was ready for him, he slipped inside and made love to her not too gently but not too fiercely — but in a way that made her feel more treasured and loved than she ever had before.

* * *

MARIA SAT NEXT to Prudence the next morning as she ate a light breakfast, hoping she wouldn't ask too many questions. Fortunately when Prudence spoke, it was to ask about her plans for the day.

"Hudson and I are going to pay a call upon my parents," she said. "I am not sure what they will have heard by now regarding the earl's death, but it is past time that I inform them I am well and tell them where I have been and what will come next."

"How do you think they will accept the news?"

Maria swallowed. She had been wondering that as well but had told herself that it didn't matter. She was a grown woman and this time she was making her own decision. She had seen what happened when she allowed them to make it for her.

"I am hoping that they will be relieved enough when they see me that they will accept everything else I have to tell them," she said, stealing a glance at Hudson, who was speaking amiably with the duke across the table.

Her life could have taken so many different directions, she mused. She could have been the duke's wife, living peacefully but not happily. She could have stayed with Lord Dennison, the dutiful wife and daughter in a life of misery. Yet here she was, promised to marry a physician, and happier with that life than anything else ever could have made her.

"There is something to be said about choosing your own destiny and taking matters into your own hands, is there not?" Prudence said, and Maria turned to her, sensing that there was more to her words than it appeared on the surface. She didn't know Prudence well, but she appeared to be a woman who relied more on her own intuition than anyone else's.

"What do you mean by that?"

Prudence put her fork down and looked around the table as if to make sure that no one was listening to them.

"When it comes to the threat upon my family, I have had enough of waiting for someone else to take care of it. I have a plan. One that I believe will work."

"Is it dangerous?" Maria asked, not wanting to betray the confidence Prudence was entrusting her with, but also not wishing for Prudence to come to any harm.

"No," Prudence said, "but I have ways to discover information that Archibald and his men cannot. Trust me. All will be fine."

"Very well," Maria said, although with some hesitation. "Do be careful?"

"Not to worry," Prudence said with a mischievous smile. "I always am."

Somehow, Maria believed it. Prudence never did anything without a plan in place, and from what Juliana said, could best some of the most skilled fencers — to the point that most would not parry with her.

Maria was soon distracted, however, by the arrival of Lady Winchester, who eyed her with a look of pride. She gazed around the table, realizing that while this might not be her true family — and one she was only beginning to know — she appreciated these people and the kindness they had shown her.

One thing was for certain — she was no longer alone.

* * *

"Well," Maria sighed that night as she and Hudson sat in a corner of the duke's drawing room after dinner. They had accepted the duke and duchess' offer to remain in his London home until Hudson was able to find another place for them to live. He would likely sell his previous home once it was repaired, and in the meantime, he had finally been convinced to accept the duke's offer to borrow the money required to buy another home — for Maria, more than for himself. He would repay it once he received the insurance funds. "That was an interesting day, rather full of revelations."

"I may have slightly misjudged your parents," he admitted. "I was having a rather difficult time forgiving them for marrying you off to Dennison, but I can see they didn't truly realize the man he was."

"No." She shook her head. "And once the marriage was done, what were they to do? I was his wife, in the eyes of the law, and they couldn't change that, nor would they have been able to hide me away."

"Though I will *never* allow any such thing to happen to our child," Hudson said fiercely, and Maria smiled at him, placing a hand over his.

"I know," she said. "You will be the best father there ever was."

"I shall attempt to be so," he vowed.

"And your mother," Maria said, unable to help the teasing in her tone, "has certainly made a new life for herself, has she not?"

Hudson nodded as Maria reflected on the romantic story his mother had told them that day. A few months ago, Hudson had treated Sir Willoughby's housekeeper. As he had been speaking with her, the widowed Sir Willoughby had happened upon Mrs. Lewis, who had accompanied Hudson to the call, and had taken an interest in her.

"So now she is to be Lady Willoughby," Maria mused, and Hudson shook his head in disbelief.

"Interesting how the world works, is it not?"

"Very," she said with a smile.

Very interesting, indeed.

EPILOGUE

"That's it! Come to Papa!"

Hudson held out his arms eagerly, waiting for the tiny boy to take a few steps toward him.

His child. The one that he had always so desperately longed for was here, in his arms, now that the one-year-old had finished taking his shaky steps toward him. And he was willing to do anything to provide his child the life that he had always vowed he would.

He looked up into Maria's eyes as she stared lovingly at the pair of them. Everyone said that his son looked just like him. He would have preferred their children favor Maria — how could he not, when she was the most beautiful woman he had ever seen — but perhaps the next one would.

"I knew this rug would help a toddler."

"You did say that," he acknowledged. "You were right."

"Are you happy with our new home?" she asked now, tilting her head at him. "Was it hard to let go of the other place?"

"No," he shook his head. "Though we did have some good memories there." He smiled somewhat wolfishly at her as he remembered a few significant ones. "However, this is a home that we have built together — that this community now knows as ours. Which is more than I could ever have asked for."

He was pleased that they had been able to find the perfect place here, in the middle of Holborn, among all of the neighbors who had become like family to him. They had accepted Maria with open arms and, as much as she was learning to cook and care for a home of her own, she was grateful to be invited to eat dinner at Hudson's patients' homes as often as they ate in their own.

"I best go prepare for tonight, if you do not mind caring for him for a moment," she said now, a smile on her face as she watched Hudson and their son together.

"Mind? Never," he said vehemently.

"Your family should all be here shortly."

"All of them are coming? Are you sure?"

"All of them," she confirmed.

"My mother and Sir Willoughby?"

"Of course."

"Even the dowager duchess?"

"Even the dowager duchess."

"What about Prudence and her husband?"

Maria hesitated.

"Prudence will be here. As for her husband — well, you know how he is. But I suspect he will come if Prudence does."

Hudson nodded. "It shall be an interesting evening, that is for certain."

"Isn't it always?" Maria said with a laugh.

She began to walk toward the kitchen area at the back of the house where their maid had already begun preparing the meal when she stopped, turned around, and crouched down next to Hudson and the baby.

"I love you, do you know that?"

He reached up a hand and stroked the side of her face. "I love you too."

"Thank you for giving me everything I never knew I wanted."

"You have nothing to thank me for," he said with a smile of his own. "We've built this life together. And it is one I would never trade for another."

"No matter the road it took us to get here."

"No matter the road."

And with their child, one made and born of love, in their arms, they sealed their words with a kiss.

THE END

* * *

DEAR READER,

Oh, Hudson and Maria. I wasn't entirely sure how these two were going to get together — I only knew that they were. I certainly never thought that Maria would be married to anyone else for a time, but when the plot began to fall into place, it all made sense — for Maria was always the woman who put the wants and needs of everyone else before herself, as she had been raised to do. In fact, as much as we enjoy our plucky heroines with minds of their own, most women of the day did exactly as they were told. Of course, Maria finally reached the point where it was more than she could bear — and she did what she needed to do in order to keep herself safe.

I know the subject matter of this book includes some heavy elements, and all that Maria faced is, unfortunately, a reality for many women. While today, in most countries, a woman is no longer the property of a man and there are people and organizations that can help, such situations are still nearly as common as they ever were, and I hope anyone in need can find the assistance they are searching for.

As for Hudson, he had much to overcome in all of his own insecurities about his past and his upbringing. He is a physician, and physicians of the day were gentlemen, much different from surgeons, who did the hands-on work of the body. Physicians typically assessed their patients without touching them and then sent them to the apothecary for their prescriptions. Hudson does a bit more than this, but it was certainly interesting to learn more about how medical treatment has changed over the years.

Our mystery, of course, is still ongoing, and I enjoy hearing from readers and your suspicions as to just who could be threatening the duke's family. In the next book our mystery will come to a resolution, but how? We will find out very soon! What role will Prudence play in uncovering the murderer? And is Lord Trundelle as suspicious as he seems?

Find out in The Quest of the Reclusive Rogue! A preview awaits you in the following pages…

* * *

The Quest of the Reclusive Rogue
Remingtons of the Regency Book 4

CAUGHT **in a compromising position with the very man she suspects of threatening her family, will she risk scandal or agree to an arranged marriage with a monster?**

Lady Prudence Remington is tired of waiting for someone else to solve her family's problems. So she takes it upon herself to determine if the new suspect in their father's murder is truly as sinister as he seems – until all goes wrong and she finds herself in an even worse position.

Since his family was destroyed by the former Duke of Warwick, Lord Trundelle has lived with one goal – to bring down the Remington family and all who are connected to them. The last thing he needs right now is to make one of them his wife – especially when she suspects him of murder.

All Lady Prudence wants is the freedom to continue fencing under her secret identity. All Lord Trundelle wants is to complete the vow he made to his father. When the opponents clash in a ringing of swords, will they discover that they cannot live with, or without, one another?

This thrilling conclusion to the mystery within The Remingtons of the Regency is a steamy Regency romance. The series is best read in order.

THE QUEST OF THE RECLUSIVE ROGUE - CHAPTER ONE

*P*rudence stood in the shadows at the back of the room, one hand on the hilt of her sword, ready to draw it against anyone that approached.

Not that she was in any danger at the moment. But she had become rather used to being on her guard, whether it was here in the hallowed ground of Angelo's Fencing Academy or as she traversed the streets between the school and Warwick House.

She was used to the room being filled with the sound of swords clashing and men alternately gasping or cheering, a place where she always found contentment. Of course, she couldn't completely be herself, for Lady Prudence Remington should never be caught in a fencing academy – as a viewer would be horror enough but as a participant? She couldn't deny, however, that she was far more at home here among strangers who had no idea the truth of her identity than she was standing in the middle of a ballroom curtseying demurely at any gentleman who approached.

"Why are we here today?" she asked Hugo in a low voice. She typically joined in with the gentlemen who remained to watch the other matches, taking her turn when was required. But Hugo had sent her a note to arrive early, as requested by fencing master Henry Angelo himself. The room felt oddly empty, despite the rapiers on the wall, and she looked around as she waited for Mr. Angelo to arrive.

Usually she was filled with confidence when she entered Angelo's, her only fear that someone would discover who she was. There was never a doubt in her actual ability. She was well aware that she could best whoever came at her. She had dueled most men here at Angelo's and had nearly always emerged the victor.

She only wished they all knew that they had been bested by a woman.

Had Angelo finally discovered her true identity?

"Nothing to fear," Hugo murmured. "Angelo will be here any moment. It sounds as though he has someone he wanted you to take on privately."

"But who?" she asked her friend, the only man who knew all of her secrets, who understood who she was, through and through – as she did him.

"I am uncertain. Angelo said it would be a good match."

Prudence nodded as she took a breath, centering herself, before Henry Angelo walked into the room.

"Mr. Robertson. Mr. Conway. Thank you for coming."

"Of course."

"I understand this is rather unusual, but your opponent prefers private matches."

She nodded as she stepped into the center of the room, taking on her identity as Mr. Peter Robertson. She was actually rather proud that Angelo had thought of her for this match. It meant that she had finally made the name for herself that she had been striving for – even if the name was contrived. Any femineity of her features, of which she was lacking in comparison to her sister or sister-in-law, of that she was certain, was explained by her youth. She had begun as an underdog, but no longer.

As she waited for her opponent, she tried to take a deep breath, but the linen she had wrapped tightly around her breasts restrained her movements. Then a man stepped out of the shadows where she hadn't even realized he had been lurking, and into the light in front of her.

Prudence sucked in a breath. She knew this man. Not well – no one knew him well, as far as she was aware. However, all knew of his brooding, reclusive ways.

Recently she had become interested in learning more about him, for he very well could be the man who killed her father.

"Mr. Peter Robertson versus Lord Trundelle," said Mr. Angelo, before taking a step back. "Begin."

Prudence nodded to Lord Trundelle, although his presence had sent her emotions into turmoil. What was he doing here? She had heard that he excelled in the sport, but very few had ever actually seen him fence.

She stood straight on her legs, her body sideways, her head upright as she looked Lord Trundelle in the eye, trying to see something – anything – within the depths of his face. He would be a handsome man, she considered, if he didn't always look as though he was ready to murder someone.

The thought caused a shiver to run down her spine, for there was a very good chance that he had done exactly that.

But there was nothing to be gained by contemplating such things at the moment. All she could do now was best him as she knew she was capable. Her right arm hung over her thigh; her left arm bent toward her left hip as she had been taught.

She pointed her right foot toward Lord Trundelle, then, holding her sword near the hook of the scabbard, she lifted it out, keeping her eyes on Lord Trundelle as she bent her right arm and raised it to the height of her shoulder, making a circle over her head before lifting her left arm to the back and readying herself for whatever Lord Trundelle had to send toward her.

She was caught off-guard when he followed none of the same movements as she had, movements that she had been precisely taught. She had to resist glancing over toward Henry Angelo to see what his opinion was on Lord Trundelle's rather unorthodox greeting, but she couldn't risk taking her eyes off the man – here or anywhere else he might appear.

She narrowed her eyes, trying to determine if he knew who she was, but he showed no signs of recognition. Unless he had been watching their family – although she wouldn't put it past him – he had no reason to be aware of her identity.

Lord Trundelle simply lifted his sword from his scabbard and pointed it toward her.

He made no move, but stood and stared at her. Prudence finally had enough of the game and decided to place her attack.

She thrust. He parried. She thrust again, this time from the inside to the outside of his sword, but he flicked her away as though she was an annoying insect. Again and again, she made her attempts, attempts that worked every time against other opponents, but he seemed to guess each move she made. Finally, realizing she was only expending energy needlessly, Prudence sat back and waited for him to make the first move instead.

He stood, the two of them facing off against one another, neither of them moving, until her patience eventually paid off. He stepped forward, only instead of one attack, he made a series of fast movements, obviously trying to trick her. But Prudence was too quick for that. She was ready for him, countering him when he feinted inside and then attacked from the outside. His eyes flashed in some admiration, and she took that moment to turn her wrist and quickly take him offguard, the point of her sword sitting against his chest.

His admiration quickly turned to a smouldering anger, one so fierce that she almost stepped back and away, dropping her position.

When Angelo called the point, she stepped back and they began again. Only this time there was no patience, no waiting in Lord Trundelle's attack. He had obviously not appreciated being bested, even if it was just a point, which in turn heated Prudence's blood. This was a sport. It was back and forth. She had as much right to win as he did, and she was certainly going to make it so.

He would have no idea what was coming at him.

* * *

BENEDICT WAS BEING BEATEN by a fresh-faced youth.

The lad was challenging him more than any other had in some time now, though it was not often that he allowed Angelo to set up a match for him. He far preferred to practice at home or have Angelo come to him.

When the fencing master had told him about the phenomenon all were talking about, Benedict knew he had to see for himself if there was any truth to the rumors.

And he was certainly not inviting a stranger to his home.

He had watched as the figure had stepped into the room, brimming with the same confidence that Benedict felt when he approached a match, the confidence he wished he had in the rest of his life. This Mr. Robertson was slightly on the short side, lean and wiry. Had it been any other sport, Benedict was sure that he could have bested him with one hand.

ELLIE ST. CLAIR

But this was fencing. A sport of skill, speed, and prowess, so it was impossible to count anyone out.

Benedict, however, possessed more skill, speed, and prowess than most others, so he didn't think he would have any issue. He had been wrong.

Robertson had obviously been taught by Angelo, or a pupil of his, using all of his techniques to begin the match, but where Benedict had thought he would continue to be predictable, the man had surprised him, seemingly understanding each of Benedict's next moves. He had a grace and ease of movement that reminded Benedict of a dance, and the more he parried and attacked, the more Benedict had the feeling that something about this man wasn't right.

He couldn't have said why the niggling doubt was taunting him, for it made so little sense even to him that he could not properly explain it.

Benedict pushed aside the thought as Robertson waited for him to attack again, but this time Benedict held back. He was always at his best when he could wait and parry, and then when his opponent tired, make his move to defeat him.

Robertson, however, kept himself so closed off and was of such sligh build that it made it difficult to find a point for his blade.

Until finally – there. He extended his sword within and nicked the man's shoulder, accidentally causing a tear in the fabric of his shirt right beside where his vest covered him. The man jumped back in alarm, bringing a hand to his shoulder as though his flesh had been nicked by the blade, even though Benedict knew that was an impossibility.

Angelo called a halt in play.

"Robertson? Is all well, man?"

"Yes," Robertson said in a grunt as his friend leaned forward in his seat as though he was about to jump up and protect him. "I—I must forfeit."

"Forfeit?" Angelo cried, his expression darkening. "Surely not. You are near to winning."

"No," Benedict agreed firmly. "You cannot."

For even if Robertson would technically lose by forfeiting the match, Benedict would be well aware that he had won only by default. Which did not sit well with him. Not at all. He had to win, and he had to win by his own merit.

"I must," Robertson said in a voice slightly more panicked and high-pitched as he backed away, still holding up his shirt material on his shoulder, which made no sense at all to Benedict. "A rematch, perhaps?"

"No," Benedict said again, more firmly this time. "We will finish this."

"I must go," Robertson with a desperate glance toward the man who had sat watching them. He immediately jumped up and nodded.

"Apologies, Lord Trundelle. Angelo. We shall see you again."

Angelo crossed his arms over his chest, seeming as dismayed as Benedict at the interruption of the match.

"I won't forget this, Robertson," he said, shaking his head.

"I understand," was all he said before nearly fleeing from the room, leaving Benedict and Angelo staring after him in dismay and incredulity.

* * *

You can find The Quest of the Reclusive Rogue on Amazon and in Kindle Unlimited!

ALSO BY ELLIE ST. CLAIR

The Remingtons
The Mystery of the Debonair Duke
The Secret of the Dashing Detective
The Clue of the Brilliant Bastard
The Quest of the Reclusive Rogue

To the Time of the Highlanders
A Time to Wed
A Time to Love
A Time to Dream

Thieves of Desire
The Art of Stealing a Duke's Heart
A Jewel for the Taking
A Prize Worth Fighting For
Gambling for the Lost Lord's Love
Romance of a Robbery

The Bluestocking Scandals
Designs on a Duke
Inventing the Viscount
Discovering the Baron
The Valet Experiment
Writing the Rake
Risking the Detective
A Noble Excavation

A Gentleman of Mystery

The Bluestocking Scandals Box Set: Books 1-4
The Bluestocking Scandals Box Set: Books 5-8

Blooming Brides
A Duke for Daisy
A Marquess for Marigold
An Earl for Iris
A Viscount for Violet

The Blooming Brides Box Set: Books 1-4

Happily Ever After
The Duke She Wished For
Someday Her Duke Will Come
Once Upon a Duke's Dream
He's a Duke, But I Love Him
Loved by the Viscount
Because the Earl Loved Me

Happily Ever After Box Set Books 1-3
Happily Ever After Box Set Books 4-6

The Victorian Highlanders
Duncan's Christmas - (prequel)
Callum's Vow
Finlay's Duty
Adam's Call
Roderick's Purpose
Peggy's Love

The Victorian Highlanders Box Set Books 1-5

Searching Hearts

Duke of Christmas (prequel)

Quest of Honor

Clue of Affection

Hearts of Trust

Hope of Romance

Promise of Redemption

Searching Hearts Box Set (Books 1-5)

Standalones

Always Your Love

The Stormswept Stowaway

A Touch of Temptation

Christmastide with His Countess

Her Christmas Wish

Merry Misrule

A Match Made at Christmas

For a full list of all of Ellie's books, please see

www.elliestclair.com/books.

ABOUT THE AUTHOR

Ellie has always loved reading, writing, and history. For many years she has written short stories, non-fiction, and has worked on her true love and passion -- romance novels.

In every era there is the chance for romance, and Ellie enjoys exploring many different time periods, cultures, and geographic locations. No matter when or where, love can always prevail. She has a particular soft spot for the bad boys of history, and loves a strong heroine in her stories.

Ellie and her husband love nothing more than spending time at home with their children and Husky cross. Ellie can typically be found at the lake in the summer, pushing the stroller all year round, and, of course, with her computer in her lap or a book in hand.

She also loves corresponding with readers, so be sure to contact her!

www.elliestclair.com
ellie@elliestclair.com

Ellie St. Clair's Ever Afters Facebook Group